A
BEAR CALLED PADDINGTON

A
Bear Called
Paddington

By

MICHAEL BOND

With drawings by
Peggy Fortnum

HOUGHTON MIFFLIN COMPANY BOSTON

Library of Congress Catalog Card Number: 60-9096
ISBN 0-395-06636-0

Printed in the United States of America

HAD   25 24 23 22

CONTENTS

CHAPTER ONE

Please Look After this Bear

MR. AND Mrs. Brown first met Paddington on a railway platform. In fact, that was how he came to have such an unusual name for a bear, for Paddington was the name of the station.

The Browns were there to meet their daughter Judy, who was coming home from school for the holidays. It was a warm summer day and the station was crowded with people on their way to the seaside. Trains were whistling, taxis hooting, porters rushing about shouting at one another, and altogether there was so much noise that Mr. Brown, who saw him first, had to tell his wife several times before she understood.

"A *bear*? On Paddington station?" Mrs. Brown looked at her husband in amazement. "Don't be silly, Henry. There can't be!"

Mr. Brown adjusted his glasses. "But there is," he insisted. "I distinctly saw it. Over there—behind those mailbags. It was wearing a funny kind of hat."

Without waiting for a reply he caught hold of his wife's arm and pushed her through the crowd, round a trolley laden with chocolate and cups of tea, past a bookstall, and through a gap in a pile of suitcases towards the Lost Property Office.

"There you are," he announced, triumphantly, pointing towards a dark corner. "I told you so!"

Mrs. Brown followed the direction of his arm and dimly made out a small, furry object in the shadows. It seemed to be sitting on some kind of suitcase and around its neck there was a label with some writing on it. The suitcase was old and battered and on the side, in large letters, were the words WANTED ON VOYAGE.

Mrs. Brown clutched at her husband. "Why, Henry," she exclaimed. "I believe you were right after all. It *is* a bear!"

She peered at it more closely. It seemed a very

unusual kind of bear. It was brown in colour, a rather dirty brown, and it was wearing a most odd-looking hat, with a wide brim, just as Mr. Brown had said. From beneath the brim two large, round eyes stared back at her.

Seeing that something was expected of it the bear stood up and politely raised its hat, revealing two black ears. " Good afternoon," it said, in a small, clear voice.

" Er . . . good afternoon," replied Mr. Brown, doubtfully. There was a moment of silence.

The bear looked at them inquiringly. " Can I help you? "

Mr. Brown looked rather embarrassed. " Well . . . no. Er . . . as a matter of fact, we were wondering if we could help you."

Mrs. Brown bent down. " You're a very small bear," she said.

The bear puffed out its chest. " I'm a very rare sort of bear," he replied, importantly. " There aren't many of us left where I come from."

" And where is that? " asked Mrs. Brown.

The bear looked round carefully before replying. " Darkest Peru. I'm not really supposed to be here at all. I'm a stowaway! "

" A stowaway? " Mr. Brown lowered his voice and looked anxiously over his shoulder. He almost expected to see a policeman standing behind him with a notebook and pencil, taking everything down.

9

"Yes," said the bear. "I emigrated, you know."
A sad expression came into its eyes. "I used to live
with my Aunt Lucy in Peru, but she had to go into
a home for retired bears."

"You don't mean to say you've come all the way
from South America by yourself?" exclaimed Mrs.
Brown.

The bear nodded. "Aunt Lucy always said she
wanted me to emigrate when I was old enough.
That's why she taught me to speak English."

"But whatever did you do for food?" asked Mr.
Brown. "You must be starving."

Bending down, the bear unlocked the suitcase with
a small key, which it also had round its neck, and
brought out an almost empty glass jar. "I ate
marmalade," he said, rather proudly. "Bears like
marmalade. And I lived in a lifeboat."

"But what are you going to do now?" said Mr.
Brown. "You can't just sit on Paddington station
waiting for something to happen."

"Oh, I shall be all right . . . I expect." The bear
bent down to do up its case again. As he did so
Mrs. Brown caught a glimpse of the writing on the
label. It said, simply, PLEASE LOOK AFTER THIS BEAR.
THANK YOU.

She turned appealingly to her husband. "Oh,
Henry, what *shall* we do? We can't just leave him
here. There's no knowing what might happen to him.
London's such a big place when you've nowhere to

go. Can't he come and stay with us for a few days?"

Mr. Brown hesitated. "But Mary, dear, we can't take him . . . not just like that. After all . . ."

"After all, *what*?" Mrs. Brown's voice had a firm note to it. She looked down at the bear. "He *is* rather sweet. And he'd be such company for Jonathan and Judy. Even if it's only for a little while. They'd never forgive you if they knew you'd left him here."

"It all seems highly irregular," said Mr. Brown, doubtfully. "I'm sure there's a law about it." He bent down. "Would you like to come and stay with us?" he asked. "That is," he added, hastily, not wishing to offend the bear, "if you've nothing else planned."

The bear jumped and his hat nearly fell off with excitement. "Oooh, yes, please. I should like that very much. I've nowhere to go and everyone seems in such a hurry."

"Well, that's settled then," said Mrs. Brown, before her husband could change his mind. "And you can have marmalade for breakfast every morning, and——" she tried hard to think of something else that bears might like.

"*Every* morning?" The bear looked as if it could hardly believe its ears. "I only had it on special occasions at home. Marmalade's very expensive in Darkest Peru."

"Then you shall have it every morning starting

to-morrow," continued Mrs. Brown. "And honey on Sunday."

A worried expression came over the bear's face. "Will it cost very much?" he asked. "You see, I haven't very much money."

"Of course not. We wouldn't dream of charging you anything. We shall expect you to be one of the family, shan't we, Henry?" Mrs. Brown looked at her husband for support.

"Of course," said Mr. Brown. "By the way," he added, "if you *are* coming home with us you'd better know our names. This is Mrs. Brown and I'm Mr. Brown."

The bear raised its hat politely—twice. "I haven't really got a name," he said. "Only a Peruvian one which no one can understand."

"Then we'd better give you an English one," said Mrs. Brown. "It'll make things much easier." She looked round the station for inspiration. "It ought to be something special," she said thoughtfully. As she spoke an engine standing in one of the platforms gave a loud whistle and let off a cloud of steam. "I know what!" she exclaimed. "We found you on Paddington station so we'll call you Paddington!"

"Paddington!" The bear repeated it several times to make sure. "It seems a very long name."

"Quite distinguished," said Mr. Brown. "Yes, I like Paddington as a name. Paddington it shall be."

Mrs. Brown stood up. " Good. Now, Paddington, I have to meet our little daughter, Judy, off the train. She's coming home from school. I'm sure you must be thirsty after your long journey, so you go along to the buffet with Mr. Brown and he'll buy you a nice cup of tea."

Paddington licked his lips. " I'm *very* thirsty," he said. " Sea water makes you thirsty." He picked up his suitcase, pulled his hat down firmly over his head, and waved a paw politely in the direction of the buffet. " After you, Mr. Brown."

" Er . . . thank you, Paddington," said Mr. Brown.

" Now, Henry, look after him," Mrs. Brown called after them. " And for goodness' sake, when you get a moment, take that label off his neck. It makes him look like a parcel. I'm sure he'll get put in a luggage van or something if a porter sees him."

The buffet was crowded when they entered but Mr. Brown managed to find a table for two in a corner. By standing on a chair Paddington could just rest his paws comfortably on the glass top. He looked around with interest while Mr. Brown went to fetch the tea. The sight of everyone eating reminded him of how hungry he felt. There was a half-eaten bun on the table but just as he reached out his paw a waitress came up and swept it into a pan.

" You don't want that, dearie," she said, giving him a friendly pat. " You don't know where it's been."

Paddington felt so empty he didn't really mind

13

where it had been but he was much too polite to say anything.

"Well, Paddington," said Mr. Brown, as he placed two steaming cups of tea on the table and a plate piled high with cakes. "How's that to be going on with?"

Paddington's eyes glistened. "It's very nice, thank you," he exclaimed, eyeing the tea doubtfully. "But it's rather hard drinking out of a cup. I usually get my head stuck, or else my hat falls in and makes it taste nasty."

Mr. Brown hesitated. "Then you'd better give your hat to me. I'll pour the tea into a saucer for you. It's not really done in the best circles, but I'm sure no one will mind just this once."

Paddington removed his hat and laid it carefully on the table while Mr. Brown poured out the tea. He looked hungrily at the cakes, in particular at a large cream-and-jam one which Mr. Brown placed on a plate in front of him.

"There you are, Paddington," he said. "I'm sorry they haven't any marmalade ones, but they were the best I could get."

"I'm glad I emigrated," said Paddington, as he reached out a paw and pulled the plate nearer. "Do you think anyone would mind if I stood on the table to eat?"

Before Mr. Brown could answer he had climbed up and placed his right paw firmly on the bun. It was a

very large bun, the biggest and stickiest Mr. Brown
had been able to find, and in a matter of moments
most of the inside found its way on to Paddington's
whiskers. People started to nudge each other and

began staring in their direction. Mr. Brown wished
he had chosen a plain, ordinary bun, but he wasn't
very experienced in the ways of bears. He stirred his
tea and looked out of the window, pretending he had
tea with a bear on Paddington station every day of
his life.

"Henry!" The sound of his wife's voice brought
him back to earth with a start. "Henry, whatever

are you doing to that poor bear? Look at him! He's covered all over with cream and jam."

Mr. Brown jumped up in confusion. " He seemed rather hungry," he answered, lamely.

Mrs. Brown turned to her daughter. " This is what happens when I leave your father alone for five minutes."

Judy clapped her hands excitedly. " Oh, Daddy, is he really going to stay with us? "

" If he does," said Mrs. Brown, " I can see someone other than your father will have to look after him. Just look at the mess he's in! "

Paddington, who all this time had been too interested in his bun to worry about what was going on, suddenly became aware that people were talking about him. He looked up to see that Mrs. Brown had been joined by a little girl, with laughing blue eyes and long, fair hair. He jumped up, meaning to raise his hat, and in his haste slipped on a patch of strawberry jam which somehow or other had found its way on to the glass table-top. For a brief moment he had a dizzy impression of everything and everyone being upside down. He waved his paws wildly in the air and then, before anyone could catch him, he somersaulted backwards and landed with a splash in his saucer of tea. He jumped up even quicker than he had sat down, because the tea was still very hot, and promptly stepped into Mr. Brown's cup.

Judy threw back her head and laughed until the

tears rolled down her face. "Oh, Mummy, isn't he funny!" she cried.

Paddington, who didn't think it at all funny, stood for a moment with one foot on the table and the other in Mr. Brown's tea. There were large patches of white cream all over his face, and on his left ear there was a lump of strawberry jam.

"You wouldn't think," said Mrs. Brown, "that anyone could get in such a state with just one bun."

Mr. Brown coughed. He had just caught the stern eye of a waitress on the other side of the counter. "Perhaps," he said, "we'd better go. I'll see if I can find a taxi." He picked up Judy's belongings and hurried outside.

Paddington stepped gingerly off the table and, with a last look at the sticky remains of his bun, climbed down on to the floor.

Judy took one of his paws. " Come along, Paddington. We'll take you home and you can have a nice hot bath. Then you can tell me all about South America. I'm sure you must have had lots of wonderful adventures."

" I have," said Paddington, earnestly. " Lots. Things are always happening to me. I'm that sort of bear."

When they came out of the buffet Mr. Brown had already found a taxi and he waved them across. The driver looked hard at Paddington and then at the inside of his nice, clean taxi.

" Bears is sixpence extra," he said, gruffly. " Sticky bears is ninepence! "

" He can't help being sticky, driver," said Mr. Brown. " He's just had a nasty accident."

The driver hesitated. " All right, 'op in. But mind none of it comes off on me interior. I only cleaned it out this morning."

The Browns trooped obediently into the back of the taxi. Mr. and Mrs. Brown and Judy sat in the back, while Paddington stood on a tip-up seat behind the driver so that he could see out of the window.

The sun was shining as they drove out of the station and after the gloom and the noise everything seemed bright and cheerful. They swept past a group of people at a bus stop and Paddington waved. Several people stared and one man raised his hat in return. It was all very friendly. After weeks of sitting alone in a lifeboat there was so much to see. There were people and cars and big, red buses everywhere—it wasn't a bit like Darkest Peru.

Paddington kept one eye out of the window in case he missed anything. With his other eye he carefully examined Mr. and Mrs. Brown and Judy. Mr. Brown was fat and jolly, with a big moustache and glasses, while Mrs. Brown, who was also rather plump, looked like a larger edition of Judy. Paddington had just decided he was going to like staying with the Browns when the glass window behind the driver shot back and a gruff voice said, " Where did you say you wanted to go ? "

Mr. Brown leaned forward. " Number thirty-two, Windsor Gardens."

The driver cupped his ear with one hand. " Can't 'ear you," he shouted.

Paddington tapped him on the shoulder. " Number thirty-two, Windsor Gardens," he repeated.

The taxi driver jumped at the sound of Paddington's voice and narrowly missed hitting a bus. He looked down at his shoulder and glared. " Cream ! " he said, bitterly. " All over me new coat ! "

Judy giggled and Mr. and Mrs. Brown exchanged glances. Mr. Brown peered at the meter. He half expected to see a sign go up saying they had to pay another sixpence.

" I beg your pardon," said Paddington. He bent forward and tried to rub the stain off with his other paw. Several bun crumbs and a smear of jam added themselves mysteriously to the taxi driver's coat. The driver gave Paddington a long, hard look. Paddington raised his hat and the driver slammed the window shut again.

" Oh dear," said Mrs. Brown. " We really shall have to give him a bath as soon as we get indoors. It's getting everywhere."

Paddington looked thoughtful. It wasn't so much that he didn't like baths; he really didn't mind being covered with jam and cream. It seemed a pity to wash it all off quite so soon. But before he had time to consider the matter the taxi stopped and the Browns began to climb out. Paddington picked up his suitcase and followed Judy up a flight of white steps to a big green door.

" Now you're going to meet Mrs. Bird," said Judy. " She looks after us. She's a bit fierce sometimes and she grumbles a lot but she doesn't really mean it. I'm sure you'll like her."

Paddington felt his knees begin to tremble. He looked round for Mr. and Mrs. Brown, but they appeared to be having some sort of argument with the taxi driver. Behind the door he could hear footsteps approaching.

"I'm sure I shall like her, if you say so," he said, catching sight of his reflection on the brightly polished letter-box. "But will she like me?"

CHAPTER TWO

A Bear in Hot Water

PADDINGTON WASN'T quite sure what to expect when Mrs. Bird opened the door. He was pleasantly surprised when they were greeted by a stout, motherly lady with grey hair and a kindly twinkle in her eyes. When she saw Judy she raised her hands above her head. " Goodness gracious, you've arrived already," she said, in horror. " And me hardly finished the washing up. I suppose you'll be wanting tea? "

" Hallo, Mrs. Bird," said Judy. " It's nice to see you again. How's the rheumatism? "

" Worse than it's ever been," began Mrs. Bird—

then she stopped speaking and stared at Paddington.
" Whatever have you got there? " she asked. " What
is it? "

" It's not a *what*," said Judy. " It's a bear. His
name's Paddington."

Paddington raised his hat.

" A *bear*," said Mrs. Bird, doubtfully. " Well, he
has good manners, I'll say that for him."

" He's going to stay with us," announced Judy.
" He's emigrated from South America and he's all
alone with nowhere to go."

" Going to *stay* with us? " Mrs. Bird raised her
arms again. " How long for? "

Judy looked round mysteriously before replying.
" I don't know," she said. " It depends on *things*."

" Mercy me," exclaimed Mrs. Bird. " I wish
you'd told me. I haven't put clean sheets in the spare
room or anything." She looked down at Paddington.
" Though judging by the state he's in perhaps that's
as well! "

" It's all right, Mrs. Bird," said Paddington. " I
think I'm going to have a bath. I had an accident
with a bun."

" Oh! " Mrs. Bird held the door open. " Oh,
well in that case you'd best come on in. Only mind
the carpet. It's just been done."

Judy took hold of Paddington's paw and squeezed.
" She doesn't mind really," she whispered. " I think
she rather likes you."

23

Paddington watched the retreating figure of Mrs. Bird. " She seems a bit fierce," he said.

Mrs. Bird turned. " What was that you said? "

Paddington jumped. " I . . . I . . ." he began.

" Where was it you said you'd come from? Peru? "

" That's right," said Paddington. " Darkest Peru."

" Humph! " Mrs. Bird looked thoughtful for a moment. " Then I expect you like marmalade. I'd better get some more from the grocer."

" There you are! What did I tell you? " cried Judy, as the door shut behind Mrs. Bird. " She *does* like you."

" Fancy her knowing I like marmalade," said Paddington.

" Mrs. Bird knows everything about everything," said Judy. " Now, you'd better come upstairs with me and I'll show you your room. It used to be mine when I was small and it has lots of pictures of bears round the wall so I expect you'll feel at home." She led the way up a long flight of stairs, chattering all the time. Paddington followed closely behind, keeping carefully to the side so that he didn't have to tread on the carpet.

" That's the bathroom," said Judy. " And that's my room. And that's Jonathan's—he's my brother, and you'll meet him soon. And that's Mummy and Daddy's." She opened a door. " And this is going to be yours! "

Paddington nearly fell over with surprise when he

followed her into the room. He'd never seen such a big one. There was a large bed with white sheets against one wall and several big boxes, one with a mirror on it. Judy pulled open a drawer in one of the boxes. " This is called a chest of drawers," she said. " You'll be able to keep all your things in here."

Paddington looked at the drawer and then at his suitcase. " I don't seem to have very much. That's the trouble with being small—no one ever expects you to want things."

" Then we shall have to see what we can do," said Judy, mysteriously. " I'll try and get Mummy to take you on one of her shopping expeditions." She knelt down beside him. " Let me help you to unpack."

" It's very kind of you," Paddington fumbled with the lock. " But I don't think there's much to help me with. There's a jar of marmalade—only there's hardly any left now and what there is tastes of sea-weed. And my scrapbook. And some centavos— they're a sort of South American penny."

" Gosh! " said Judy. " I've never seen any of those before. Aren't they bright! "

" Oh, I keep them polished," said Paddington. " I don't *spend* them." He pulled out a tattered photograph. " And that's a picture of my Aunt Lucy. She had it taken just before she went into the home for retired bears in Lima."

" She looks very nice," said Judy. " And very wise." Seeing that Paddington had a sad, far-away look in his eyes, she added hastily, " Well, I'm going to leave you now, so that you can have your bath and come down nice and clean. You'll find two taps, one marked hot and one marked cold. There's plenty of soap and a clean towel. Oh, and a brush so that you can scrub your back."

" It sounds very complicated," said Paddington. " Can't I just sit in a puddle or something ? "

Judy laughed. " Somehow I don't think Mrs. Bird would approve of that! And don't forget to wash your ears. They look awfully black."

" They're meant to be black," Paddington called indignantly, as Judy shut the door.

He climbed up on to a stool by the window and looked out. There was a large, interesting garden below, with a small pond and several trees which looked good for climbing. Beyond the trees he could see some more houses stretching away into the distance. He decided it must be wonderful living in a house like this all the time. He stayed where he was, thinking about it, until the window became steamed up and he couldn't see out any more. Then he tried writing his name on the cloudy part with his paws. He began to wish it wasn't quite so long, as he soon ran out of cloud and it was rather difficult to spell.

" All the same "—he climbed on to the dressing-table and looked at himself in the mirror—" it's a very important name. I don't expect there are many bears in the world called Paddington! "

If he'd only known, Judy was saying exactly the same thing to Mr. Brown at that very moment. The Browns were holding a council of war in the dining-room, and Mr. Brown was fighting a losing battle. It had been Judy's idea in the first place to keep Paddington. In this she not only had Jonathan on her side but also her Mother. Jonathan had yet to meet Paddington but the idea of having a bear in the family appealed to him. It sounded very important.

"After all, Henry," argued Mrs. Brown, "you can't turn him out now. It wouldn't be right."

Mr. Brown sighed. He knew when he was beaten. It wasn't that he didn't like the idea of keeping Paddington. Secretly he was just as keen as anyone. But as head of the Brown household he felt he ought to consider the matter from every angle.

"I'm sure we ought to report the matter to someone first," he said.

"I don't see why, Dad," cried Jonathan. "Besides, he might get arrested for being a stowaway if we do that."

Mrs. Brown put down her knitting. "Jonathan's right, Henry. We can't let that happen. It's not as if he's done anything wrong. I'm sure he didn't harm anyone travelling in a lifeboat like that."

"Then there's the question of pocket money," said Mr. Brown, weakening. "I'm not sure how much pocket-money to give a bear."

" He can have one and sixpence a week, the same as the other children," replied Mrs. Brown.

Mr. Brown lit his pipe carefully before replying. " Well," he said, " we'll have to see what Mrs. Bird has to say about it first, of course."

There was a triumphant chorus from the rest of the family.

" You'd better ask her then," said Mrs. Brown, when the noise had died down. " It was your idea."

Mr. Brown coughed. He was a little bit afraid of Mrs. Bird and he wasn't at all sure how she would take it. He was about to suggest they left it for a little while when the door opened and Mrs. Bird herself came in with the tea things. She paused for a moment and looked round at the sea of expectant faces.

" I suppose," she said, " you want to tell me you've decided to keep that young Paddington."

" May we, Mrs. Bird? " pleaded Judy. " *Please!* I'm sure he'll be very good."

" Humph! " Mrs. Bird put the tray down on the table. " That remains to be seen. Different people have different ideas about being good. All the same," she hesitated at the door. " He looks the sort of bear that means well."

" Then you don't mind, Mrs. Bird? " Mr. Brown. asked her.

Mrs. Bird thought for a moment. " No. No, I don't mind at all. I've always had a soft spot for bears myself. It'll be nice to have one about the house."

" Well," gasped Mrs. Brown, as the door closed. " Whoever would have thought it! "

" I expect it was because he raised his hat," said Judy. " It made a good impression. Mrs. Bird likes polite people."

Mrs. Brown picked up her knitting again. " I suppose someone ought to write and tell his Aunt Lucy. I'm sure she'd like to know he's safe." She turned to Judy. "Perhaps it would be a nice thought if you and Jonathan wrote."

" By the way," said Mr. Brown, " come to think of it, where *is* Paddington? He's not still up in his room, is he? "

Judy looked up from the writing-desk, where she was searching for some notepaper. " Oh, he's all right. He's just having a bath."

" A *bath*! " Mrs. Brown's face took on a worried expression. " He's rather small to be having a bath all by himself."

" Don't fuss so, Mary," grumbled Mr. Brown, settling himself down in the armchair with a news-paper. " He's probably having the time of his life."

Mr. Brown was fairly near the truth when he said Paddington was probably having the time of his life. Unfortunately it wasn't in quite the way he meant it. Blissfully unaware that his fate was being decided, Paddington was sitting in the middle of the bathroom floor drawing a map of South America with a tube of Mr. Brown's shaving cream.

Paddington liked geography. At least, he liked *his* sort of geography, which meant seeing strange places and new people. Before he left South America on his long journey to England, his Aunt Lucy, who was a very wise old bear, had done her best to teach him all she knew. She had told him all about the places he would see on the way and she had spent many long hours reading to him about the people he would meet.

It had been a long journey, half-way round the world, and so Paddington's map occupied most of the bathroom floor and also used up most of Mr. Brown's shaving cream. With the little that was left he tried writing his new name again. He had several attempts and finally decided on PADINGTUN. It looked most important.

It wasn't until a trickle of warm water landed on his nose that he realised the bath was full and was beginning to run over the side. With a sigh he climbed up on to the side of the bath, closed his eyes, held his nose with one paw, and jumped. The water was hot and soapy and much deeper than he had expected. In fact, he had to stand on tiptoe even to keep his nose above the surface.

It was then that he had a nasty shock. It's one thing getting into a bath. It's quite another matter getting out, especially when the water comes up to your nose and the sides are slippery and your eyes are full of soap. He couldn't even see to turn the taps off.

He tried calling out " Help," first in quite a quiet

voice, then very loudly: "HELP! HELP!"

He waited for a few moments but no one came. Suddenly he had an idea. What a good thing he was still wearing his hat! He took it off and began baling out the water.

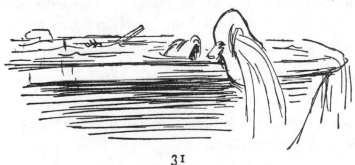

There were several holes in the hat because it was a very old one that had once belonged to his uncle, but if the water didn't get much less, at least it didn't get any more.

"That's funny," said Mr. Brown, jumping up from his armchair and rubbing his forehead. "I could have sworn I felt a spot of water!"

"Don't be silly, dear. How could you?" Mrs. Brown, busy with her knitting didn't even bother to look up.

Mr. Brown grunted and returned to his newspaper. He *knew* he had felt something, but there was no point in arguing. He looked suspiciously at the children, but both Judy and Jonathan were busy writing their letter.

"How much does it cost to send a letter to Lima?" asked Jonathan.

Judy was about to reply when another drop of water fell down from the ceiling, this time right on to the table.

"Oh, gosh!" she jumped to her feet, pulling Jonathan after her. There was an ominous wet patch right over their heads *and* right underneath the bathroom!

"Where are you going now, dear?" asked Mrs. Brown.

"Oh, just upstairs to see how Paddington's getting on." Judy pushed Jonathan through the door and shut it quickly behind them.

" Crikey," said Jonathan. " What's up? "

" It's Paddington," cried Judy over her shoulder as she rushed up the stairs. " I think he's in trouble! "

She ran along the landing and banged loudly on the bathroom door. " Are you all right, Paddington? " she shouted. " May we come in? "

" HELP! HELP! " shouted Paddington. " *Please* come in. I think I'm going to drown! "

" Oh, Paddington," Judy leant over the side of the bath and helped Jonathan lift a dripping and very frightened Paddington on to the floor. " Oh, Paddington! Thank goodness you're all right! "

Paddington lay on his back in a pool of water. " What a good job I had my hat," he panted. " Aunt Lucy told me never to be without it."

" But why on earth didn't you pull the plug out, you silly? " said Judy.

" Oh! " Paddington looked crestfallen. " I . . . I never thought of that."

Jonathan looked admiringly at Paddington. " Crikey," he said. " Fancy you making all this mess. Even *I've* never made as much mess as this! "

Paddington sat up and looked around. The whole of the bathroom floor was covered in a sort of white foam where the hot water had landed on his map of South America. " It *is* a bit untidy," he admitted. " I don't really know how it got like that."

" Untidy! " Judy lifted him to his feet and wrapped

33

a towel around him. " Paddington, we've all got a lot of work to do before we go downstairs again. If Mrs. Bird sees this I don't know what she'll say."

" I do," exclaimed Jonathan. " She says it to me sometimes."

Judy began wiping the floor with a cloth. " Now

just you dry yourself quickly in case you catch cold."

Paddington began rubbing himself meekly with the towel. " I must say," he remarked, looking at himself in the mirror. " I *am* a lot cleaner than I was. It doesn't look like me at all! "

Paddington *did* look much cleaner than when he had first arrived at the Browns. His fur, which was really quite light in colour and not dark brown as it had been, was standing out like a new brush, except

34

that it was soft and silky. His nose gleamed and his ears had lost all traces of the jam and cream. He was so much cleaner that when he arrived downstairs and entered the dining-room some time later, everyone pretended not to recognise him.

"The tradesmen's entrance is at the side," said Mr. Brown, from behind his paper.

Mrs. Brown put down her knitting and stared at him. "I think you must have come to the wrong house," she said. "This is number thirty-two not thirty-four!"

Even Jonathan and Judy agreed there must be some mistake. Paddington began to get quite worried until they all burst out laughing and said how nice he looked now that he was brushed and combed and respectable.

They made room for him in a small armchair by the fire and Mrs. Bird came in with another pot of tea and a plate of hot, buttered toast.

"Now, Paddington," said Mr. Brown, when they were all settled. "Suppose you tell us all about yourself and how you came to Britain."

Paddington settled back in his armchair, wiped a smear of butter carefully from his whiskers, put his paws behind his head and stretched out his toes towards the fire. He liked an audience, especially when he was warm and the world seemed such a nice place.

"I was brought up in Darkest Peru," he began.

" By my Aunt Lucy. She's the one that lives in a home for retired bears in Lima." He closed his eyes thoughtfully.

A hush fell over the room and everyone waited expectantly. After a while, when nothing happened, they began to get restless. Mr. Brown coughed loudly. " It doesn't seem a very exciting story," he said, impatiently.

He reached across and poked Paddington with his pipe. " Well I never," he said. " I do believe he's fallen asleep! "

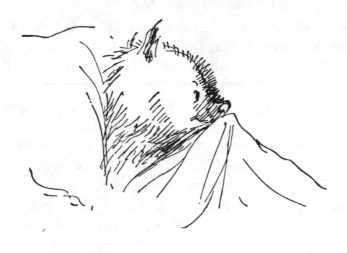

CHAPTER THREE

Paddington Goes Underground

PADDINGTON WAS very surprised when he woke up the next morning and found himself in bed. He decided it was a nice feeling as he stretched himself and pulled the sheets up round his head with a paw. He reached out with his feet and found a cool spot for his toes. One advantage of being a very small bear in a large bed was that there was so much room.

After a few minutes he poked his head out cautiously and sniffed. There was a lovely smell of something coming under the door. It seemed to be getting nearer and nearer. There were footsteps too, coming up the stairs. As they stopped by his door there was

37

a knock and Mrs. Bird's voice called out, " Are you awake, young Paddington ? "

" Only just," called out Paddington, rubbing his eyes.

The door opened. " You've had a good sleep," said Mrs. Bird as she placed a tray on the bed and drew the curtains. " And you're a very privileged person to have breakfast in bed on a *weekday*! "

Paddington eyed the tray hungrily. There was half a grapefruit in a bowl, a plate of bacon and eggs, some toast, and a whole pot of marmalade, not to mention a large cup of tea. " Is all that for me ? " he exclaimed.

" If you don't want it I can soon take it away again," said Mrs. Bird.

" Oh, I do," said Paddington, hurriedly. " It's just that I've never seen so much breakfast before."

" Well, you'd better hurry up with it." Mrs. Bird turned in the doorway and looked back. " Because you're going on a shopping expedition this morning with Mrs. Brown and Judy. And all I can say is, thank goodness I'm not going too! " She closed the door.

" Now I wonder what she meant by that ? " said Paddington. But he didn't worry about it for very long. There was far too much to do. It was the first time he had ever had breakfast in bed and he soon found it wasn't quite so easy as it looked. First of all he had trouble with the grapefruit. Every time he pressed it with his spoon a long stream of juice

shot up and hit him in the eye, which was very painful.
And all the time he was worried because the bacon
and eggs were getting cold. Then there was the
question of the marmalade. He wanted to leave
room for the marmalade.

In the end he decided it would be much easier if
he mixed everything up on the one plate and sat on
the tray to eat it.

"Oh, Paddington," said Judy when she entered
the room a few minutes later and found him perched
on the tray, "whatever are you doing now? Do
hurry up. We're waiting for you downstairs."

Paddington looked up, an expression of bliss on
his face; that part of his face which could be seen
behind eggy whiskers and toast crumbs. He tried

to say something but all he could manage was a muffled grunting noise which sounded like IMJUST-COMING all rolled into one.

"Really!" Judy took out her handkerchief and wiped his face. "You're the stickiest bear imaginable. And if you don't hurry up all the nice things will be gone. Mummy's going to buy you a complete new outfit at Barkridges — I heard her say so. Now, comb your fur quickly and come on down."

As she closed the door Paddington looked at the remains of his breakfast. Most of it was gone but there was a large piece of bacon left which it seemed a pity to waste. He decided to put it into his suitcase in case he got hungry later on.

He hurried into the bathroom and rubbed his face over with some warm water. Then he combed his whiskers carefully and a few moments later, not looking perhaps as clean as he had done the evening before, but quite smart, he arrived downstairs.

"I hope you're not wearing that hat," said Mrs. Brown, as she looked down at him.

"Oh, do let him, Mummy," cried Judy. "It's so . . . so unusual."

"It's unusual all right," said Mrs. Brown. "I don't know that I've ever seen anything quite like it before. It's such a funny shape. I don't know what you'd call it."

"It's a bush hat," said Paddington, proudly. "And it saved my life."

" Saved your life? " repeated Mrs. Brown. " Don't be silly. How could a hat save your life? "

Paddington was about to tell her of his adventure in the bath the evening before when he received a nudge from Judy. She shook her head. " Er . . . it's a long story," he said, lamely.

" Then you'd better save it for another time," said Mrs. Brown. " Now, come along, both of you."

Paddington picked up his suitcase and followed Mrs. Brown and Judy to the front door. By the door Mrs. Brown paused and sniffed.

" That's very strange," she said. " There seems to be a smell of bacon everywhere this morning. Can *you* smell it, Paddington? "

Paddington started. He put the suitcase guiltily behind himself and sniffed. He had several expressions which he kept for emergencies. There was his thoughtful expression, when he stared into space and rested his chin on a paw. Then there was his innocent one which wasn't really an expression at all. He decided to use this one.

" It's very strong," he said, truthfully, for he was a truthful bear. And then he added, perhaps not quite so truthfully, " I wonder where it's coming from? "

" If I were you," whispered Judy, as they walked along the road towards the tube station, " I should be more careful in future when you pack your suitcase! "

Paddington looked down. A large piece of bacon

41

stuck out of the side of his case and was trailing on the pavement.

" Shoo! " cried Mrs. Brown as a grubby looking dog came bounding across the road. Paddington waved his suitcase. " Go away, dog," he said, sternly. The dog licked its lips and Paddington glanced anxiously over his shoulder as he hurried on, keeping close behind Mrs. Brown and Judy.

" Oh dear," said Mrs. Brown. " I have a funny feeling about to-day. As if *things* are going to happen. Do you ever have that feeling, Paddington ? "

Paddington considered for a moment. " Sometimes," he said vaguely as they entered the station.

At first Paddington was a little bit disappointed in the Underground. He liked the noise and the bustle and the smell of warm air which greeted him as they went inside. But he didn't think much of the ticket.

He examined carefully the piece of green cardboard which he held in his paw. " It doesn't seem much to get for fourpence," he said. After all the lovely whirring and clanking noises the ticket machine had made it did seem disappointing. He'd expected much more for fourpence.

" But Paddington," Mrs. Brown sighed, " you only have a ticket so that you can ride on the train. They won't let you on otherwise." She looked and sounded rather flustered. Secretly she was beginning to wish they had waited until later in the day, when it wasn't quite so crowded. There was also the peculiar business of the dogs. Not one, but six dogs of various shapes and sizes had followed them right inside. She had a funny feeling it had something to do with Paddington, but the only time she caught his eye it had such an innocent expression she felt quite upset with herself for having such thoughts.

" I suppose," she said to Paddington, as they stepped on the escalator, " we ought really to carry you. It says you're supposed to carry dogs but it doesn't say anything about bears."

Paddington didn't answer. He was following behind in a dream. Being a very short bear he couldn't easily see over the side, but when he did his eyes nearly popped out with excitement. There were people everywhere. He'd never seen so many. There were people rushing down one side and there were more people rushing up the other. Everyone seemed in a terrible hurry. As he stepped off the escalator he found himself carried away between a man with an umbrella and a lady with a large shopping bag. By the time he managed to push his way free both Mrs. Brown and Judy had completely disappeared.

It was then that he saw a most surprising notice. He blinked at it several times to make sure but each time he opened his eyes it said the same thing: FOLLOW THE AMBER LIGHT TO PADDINGTON.

Paddington decided the Underground was quite the most exciting thing that had ever happened to him. He turned and trotted down the corridor, following the amber lights, until he met another crowd of people who were queueing for the ' up ' escalator.

" 'ere, 'ere," said the man at the top, as he examined Paddington's ticket. " What's all this? You haven't been anywhere yet! "

" I know," said Paddington, unhappily. " I think I must have made a mistake at the bottom."

The man sniffed suspiciously and called across to an inspector. " There's a young bear 'ere, smelling of bacon. Says he made a mistake at the bottom."

The inspector put his thumbs under his waistcoat. " Escalators is for the benefit and convenience of passengers," he said, sternly. " Not for the likes of young bears to play on. Especially in the rush hour."

" Yes, sir," said Paddington, raising his hat. " But we don't have esca . . . esca . . ."

" . . . lators," said the inspector, helpfully.

" . . . lators," said Paddington, " in Darkest Peru. I've never been on one before, so it's rather difficult."

" Darkest Peru? " said the inspector, looking most impressed. " Oh, well in that case "—he lifted up the chain which divided the ' up ' and the ' down ' escalators—" you'd better get back down. But don't let me catch you up to any tricks again."

" Thank you very much," said Paddington gratefully, as he ducked under the chain. " It's very kind of you, I'm sure." He turned to wave good-bye, but before he could raise his hat he found himself being whisked into the derths of the Underground again.

Half-way down he was gazing with interest at the brightly coloured posters on the wall when the man standing behind poked him with his umbrella. " There's someone calling you," he said.

Paddington looked round and was just in time to see Mrs. Brown and Judy pass by on their way up. They waved frantically at him and Mrs. Brown called out " Stop! " several times.

Paddington turned and tried to run up the escalator, but it was going very fast, and with his short legs it was as much as he could do even to stand still. He had his head down and he didn't notice a fat man with a briefcase who was running in the opposite direction until it was too late.

There was a roar of rage from the fat man and he toppled over and grabbed at several other people. Then Paddington felt himself falling. He went bump, bump, bump all the way down before he shot off the end and finally skidded to a stop by the wall.

When he looked round everything seemed very confused. A number of people were gathered round the fat man, who was sitting on the floor rubbing his head. Away in the distance he could see Mrs. Brown and Judy trying to push their way down the 'up' escalator. It was while he was watching their efforts that he saw another notice. It was in a brass case at the bottom of the escalator and it said, in big red letters: TO STOP THE ESCALATOR IN CASES OF EMERGENCY PUSH THE BUTTON.

It also said in much smaller letters, 'Penalty for Improper Use—£5.' But in his hurry Paddington did not notice this. In any case it seemed to him very much of an emergency. He swung his suitcase through the air and hit the button as hard as he could.

If there had been confusion while the escalator was moving, there was even more when it stopped. Paddington watched with surprise as everyone started running about in different directions shouting at each other. One man even began calling out 'Fire!' and somewhere in the distance a bell began to ring.

He was just thinking what a lot of excitement pressing one small button could cause when a heavy hand descended on his shoulder.

" That's him! " someone shouted, pointing an accusing finger. " Saw him do it with me own eyes. As large as life! "

" Hit it with his suitcase," shouted another voice. " Ought not to be allowed! " While from the back of the crowd someone else suggested sending for the police.

Paddington began to feel frightened. He turned and looked up at the owner of the hand.

" Oh," said a stern voice. " It's *you* again. I might have known." The inspector took out a notebook. " Name, please."

" Er . . . Paddington," said Paddington.

" I said what's your name, not where do you want to go," repeated the inspector.

" That's right," said Paddington. " That *is* my name."

" *Paddington!* " said the inspector, disbelievingly. " It can't be. That's the name of a station. I've never heard of a bear called Paddington before."

" It's very unusual," said Paddington. " But it's Paddington Brown, and I live at number thirty-two Windsor Gardens. And I've lost Mrs. Brown and Judy."

" Oh! " The inspector wrote something in his book. " Can I see your ticket? "

" Er . . . I had it," said Paddington. " But I don't seem to any more."

The inspector began writing again. " Playing on

47

the escalator. Travelling without a ticket. *Stopping*
the escalator. All serious offences they are." He
looked up. "What have you got to say to that,
young feller me lad?"

"Well . . . er . . ." Paddington shifted uneasily
and looked down at his paws.

"Have you tried looking inside your hat?" asked
the inspector, not unkindly. "People often put their
tickets in there."

Paddington jumped with relief. "I knew I had
it somewhere," he said, thankfully, as he handed it
to the inspector.

The inspector handed it back again quickly. The
inside of Paddington's hat was rather sticky.

"I've never known anyone take so long not to get
anywhere," he said, looking hard at Paddington.
"Do you often travel on the Underground?"

"It's the first time," said Paddington.

"And the last if I have anything to do with it,"
said Mrs. Brown as she pushed her way through the
crowd.

"Is this your bear, Madam," asked the inspector.
"Because if it is, I have to inform you that he's in
serious trouble." He began to read from his notebook. "As far as I can see he's broken two important
regulations—probably more. I shall have to give him
into custody."

"Oh dear." Mrs. Brown clutched at Judy for
support. "Do you *have* to? He's only small and

it's his first time out in London. I'm sure he won't do it again."

"Ignorance of the law is no excuse," said the inspector, ominously. "Not in court! Persons are expected to abide by the regulations. It says so."

"In court!" Mrs. Brown passed a hand nervously

over her forehead. The word court always upset her. She had visions of Paddington being taken away in handcuffs and being cross-examined and all sorts of awful things.

Judy took hold of Paddington's paw and squeezed it reassuringly. Paddington looked up gratefully. He wasn't at all sure what they were talking about, but none of it sounded very nice.

"Did you say *persons* are expected to abide by the regulations?" Judy asked, firmly.

49

"That's right," began the inspector. "And I have my duty to do the same as everyone else."

"But it doesn't say anything about bears?" asked Judy, innocently.

"Well," the inspector scratched his head. "Not in so many words." He looked down at Judy, then at Paddington, and then all around. The escalator had started up again and the crowd of sightseers had disappeared.

"It's all highly irregular," he said. "But . . ."

"Oh, thank you," said Judy. "I think you're the kindest man I've ever met! Don't *you* think so, Paddington?" Paddington nodded his head vigorously and the inspector blushed.

"I shall always travel on this Underground in future," said Paddington, politely. "I'm sure it's the nicest in all London."

The inspector opened his mouth and seemed about to say something, but he closed it again.

"Come along, children," said Mrs. Brown, hastily. "If we don't hurry up we shall never get our shopping done."

From somewhere up above came the sound of some dogs barking. The inspector sighed. "I can't understand it," he said. "This used to be such a well run, respectable station. Now look at it!"

He stared after the retreating figures of Mrs. Brown and Judy with Paddington bringing up the rear and then he rubbed his eyes. "That's funny," he said, more to himself. " I must be seeing things. I could have sworn that bear had some bacon sticking out of his case! " He shrugged his shoulders. There were more important things to worry about. Judging by the noise coming from the top of the escalator there was some sort of dog fight going on. It needed investigating.

CHAPTER FOUR

A Shopping Expedition

THE MAN in the gentlemen's outfitting department at Barkridges held Paddington's hat at arm's length between thumb and forefinger. He looked at it distastefully.

"I take it the young . . . er, gentleman, will not be requiring this any more, Modom?" he said.

"Oh yes, I shall," said Paddington, firmly. "I've always had that hat—ever since I was small."

"But wouldn't you like a nice new one, Paddington?" said Mrs. Brown, adding hastily, "for *best*?"

Paddington thought for a moment. "I'll have one for *worst* if you like," he said. "*That*'s my best one!"

The salesman shuddered slightly and, averting his gaze, placed the offending article in the far end of the counter.

"Albert!" He beckoned to a youth who was hovering in the background. "See what we have in size $4\frac{7}{8}$." Albert began to rummage under the counter.

"And now, while we're about it," said Mrs. Brown, "we'd like a nice warm coat for the winter. Something like a duffle coat with toggles so that he can do it up easily, I thought. And we'd also like a plastic raincoat for the summer."

The salesman looked at her haughtily. He wasn't very fond of bears and this one, especially, had been giving him queer looks ever since he'd mentioned his wretched hat. "Has Modom tried the bargain basement?" he began. "Something in Government Surplus . . ."

"No, I haven't," said Mrs. Brown, hotly. "Government Surplus indeed! I've never heard of such a thing—have you, Paddington?"

"No," said Paddington, who had no idea what Government Surplus was. "*Never!*" He stared hard at the man, who looked away uneasily. Paddington had a very persistent stare when he cared to use it. It was a very powerful stare. One which his Aunt Lucy had taught him and which he kept for special occasions.

Mrs. Brown pointed to a smart blue duffle coat with a red lining. " That looks the very thing," she said.

The assistant gulped. " Yes, Modom. Certainly, Modom." He beckoned to Paddington. " Come this way, sir."

Paddington followed the assistant, keeping about two feet behind him, and staring very hard. The back of the man's neck seemed to go a dull red and he fingered his collar nervously. As they passed the hat counter, Albert, who lived in constant fear of his superior, and who had been watching the events with an open mouth, gave Paddington the thumbs-up sign. Paddington waved a paw. He was beginning to enjoy himself.

He allowed the assistant to help him on with the coat and then stood admiring himself in the mirror. It was the first coat he had ever possessed. In Peru it had been very hot, and though his Aunt Lucy had made him wear a hat to prevent sunstroke, it had always been much too warm for a coat of any sort. He looked at himself in the mirror and was surprised to see not one, but a long line of bears stretching away as far as the eye could see. In fact, everywhere he looked there were bears, and they were all looking extremely smart.

" Isn't the hood a trifle large? " asked Mrs. Brown, anxiously.

" Hoods are being worn large this year, Modom," said the assistant. " It's the latest fashion." He was about to add that Paddington seemed to have rather a large head anyway but he changed his mind. Bears were rather unpredictable. You never quite knew what they were thinking and this one in particular seemed to have a mind of his own.

" Do *you* like it, Paddington? " asked Mrs. Brown. Paddington gave up counting bears in the mirror and turned round to look at the back view. " I think it's the nicest coat I've ever seen," he said, after a moment's thought. Mrs. Brown and the assistant heaved a sigh of relief.

" Good," said Mrs. Brown. " That's settled, then. Now there's just the question of a hat and a plastic mackintosh."

She walked over to the hat counter, where Albert, who could still hardly take his admiring eyes off Paddington, had arranged a huge pile of hats. There were bowler hats, sun hats, trilby hats, berets, and even a very small top hat. Mrs. Brown eyed them doubtfully. " It's difficult," she said, looking at Paddington. " It's largely a question of his ears. They stick out rather."

" You could cut some holes for them," said Albert.

The assistant froze him with a glance. " Cut a hole

in a *Barkridge's* hat!" he exclaimed. "I've never heard of such a thing."

Paddington turned and stared at him. "I . . . er . . ." The assistant's voice trailed off. "I'll go and fetch my scissors," he said, in a queer voice.

"I don't think that will be necessary at all," said Mrs. Brown, hurriedly. "It's not as if he had to go to work in the city, so he doesn't want anything too smart. I think this woollen beret is very nice. The one with the pom-pom on top. The green will go well with his new coat and it'll stretch so that he can pull it down over his ears when it gets cold."

Everyone agreed that Paddington looked very smart, and while Mrs. Brown looked for a plastic mackintosh, he trotted off to have another look at himself in the mirror. He found the beret was a little difficult to raise as his ears kept the bottom half firmly in place. But by pulling on the pom-pom he could make it stretch quite a long way, which was almost as good. It meant, too, that he could be polite without getting his ears cold.

The assistant wanted to wrap up the duffle coat for him but after a lot of fuss it was agreed that, even though it was a warm day, he should wear it. Paddington felt very proud of himself and he was anxious to see if other people noticed.

After shaking hands with Albert, Paddington gave the assistant one more long, hard stare and the unfortunate man collapsed into a chair and began mopping his brow as Mrs. Brown led the way out through the door.

Barkridges was a large shop and it even had its own escalator as well as several lifts. Mrs. B hesitated at the door and then took Paddington's paw firmly in her hand and led him towards the lift. She'd had enough of escalators for one day.

But to Paddington everything was new, or almost everything, and he liked trying strange things. After a few seconds he decided quite definitely that he preferred riding on an escalator. They were nice and smooth. But lifts! To start with, it was full of people carrying parcels and all so busy they had no time to notice a small bear—one woman even rested her shopping bag on his head and seemed quite surprised when Paddington pushed it off. Then, suddenly, half of him seemed to fall away while the other half stayed where it was. Just as he had got used to that feeling the second half of him caught up again and even overtook the first half before the doors opened. It did that four times on the way down and Paddington was glad when the man in charge said it was the ground floor and Mrs. Brown led him out.

She looked at him closely. " Oh dear, Paddington, you look quite pale," she said. " Are you all right ? "

" I feel sick," said Paddington. " I don't like lifts. And I wish I hadn't had such a big breakfast ! "

" Oh dear ! " Mrs. Brown looked around. Judy, who had gone off to do some shopping of her own, was nowhere to be seen. " Will you be all right sitting here for a few minutes while I go off to find Judy ? " she asked.

Paddington sank down on to his case looking very mournful. Even the pom-pom on his hat seemed limp.

" I don't know whether I shall be all right," he said. " But I'll do my best."

" I'll be as quick as I can," said Mrs. Brown. " Then we can take a taxi home for lunch."

Paddington groaned. " Poor Paddington," said Mrs. Brown, " you must be feeling bad if you don't want any lunch." At the word lunch again, Paddington closed his eyes and gave an even louder groan. Mrs. Brown tiptoed away.

Paddington kept his eyes closed for several minutes and then, as he began to feel better, he gradually became aware that every now and then a nice cool draught of air blew over his face. He opened one eye carefully to see where it was coming from and noticed for the first time that he was sitting near the main entrance to the shop. He opened his other eye and decided to investigate. If he stayed just outside the glass door he could still see Mrs. Brown and Judy when they came.

And then, as he bent down to pick up his suitcase, everything suddenly went black. " Oh dear," thought Paddington, " now all the lights have gone out."

He began groping his way with outstretched paws towards the door. He gave a push where he thought it ought to be but nothing happened. He tried moving along the wall a little way and gave another push. This time it did move. The door seemed to have a strong spring on it and he had to push hard to make it open but eventually there was a gap big enough for him to squeeze through. It clanged shut behind him and Paddington was disappointed to find it was just as dark outside as it had been in the shop. He began to wish he'd stayed where he was. He turned round and tried to find the door but it seemed to have disappeared.

He decided it might be easier if he got down on his paws and crawled. He went a little way like this and then his head came up against something hard. He tried to push it to one side with his paw and it moved slightly so he pushed again.

Suddenly, there was a noise like thunder, and before he knew where he was a whole mountain of

things began to fall on him. It felt as if the whole sky had fallen in. Everything went quiet and he lay where he was for a few minutes with his eyes tightly shut, hardly daring to breathe. From a long way away he could hear voices and once or twice it sounded as if someone was banging on a window. He opened one eye carefully and was surprised to find the lights had come on again. At least . . . Sheepishly, he pushed the hood of his duffle coat up over his head.

They hadn't gone out at all! His hood must have fallen over his head when he bent down inside the shop to pick up his case.

Paddington sat up and looked around to see where he was. He felt much better now. Somewhat to his astonishment, he found he was sitting in a small room in the middle of which was a great pile of tins and basins and bowls. He rubbed his eyes and stared, round-eyed, at the sight.

Behind him there was a wall with a door in it, and in front of him there was a large window. On the other side of the window there was a large crowd of people pushing one another and pointing in his direction. Paddington decided with pleasure that they must be pointing at him. He stood up with difficulty, because it was hard standing up straight on top of a lot of tins, and pulled the pom-pom on his hat as high as it would go. A cheer went up from the crowd. Paddington gave a bow, waved several times, and then started to examine the damage all around him.

For a moment he wasn't quite sure where he was, and then it came to him. Instead of going out into the street he must have opened a door leading to one of the shop windows!

Paddington was an observant bear, and since he had arrived in London he'd noticed lots of these shop windows. They were very interesting. They always had so many things inside them to look at.

61

Once, he'd seen a man working in one, piling tin cans and boxes on top of each other to make a pyramid. He remembered deciding at the time what a nice job it must be.

He looked round thoughtfully. " Oh dear," he said to the world in general, " I'm in trouble again." If he'd knocked all these things down, as he supposed he must have done, someone was going to be cross. In fact, lots of people were going to be cross. People weren't very good at having things explained to them and it was going to be difficult explaining how his duffle coat hood had fallen over his head.

He bent down and began to pick up the things. There were some glass shelves lying on the floor where they had fallen. It was getting warm inside the window so he took off his duffle coat and hung it carefully on a nail. Then he picked up a glass shelf and tried balancing it on top of some tins. It seemed to work so he put some more tins and a washing-up bowl on top of that. It was rather wobbly but . . . he stood back and examined it . . . yes, it looked quite nice. There was an encouraging round of applause from outside. Paddington waved a paw at the crowd and picked up another shelf.

Inside the shop, Mrs. Brown was having an earnest conversation with the store detective.

" You say you left him here, Madam? " the detective was saying.

" That's right," said Mrs. Brown. " He was

feeling ill and I *told* him not to go away. His name's
Paddington."

"Paddington." The detective wrote it carefully
in his notebook. "What sort of bear is he?"

"Oh, he's sort of golden," said Mrs. Brown. "He
was wearing a blue duffle coat and carrying a suitcase."

"And he has black ears," said Judy. "You can't
mistake him."

"Black ears," the detective repeated, licking his
pencil.

"I don't expect that'll help much," said Mrs.
Brown. "He was wearing his beret."

The detective cupped his hand over his ear. "His
what?" he shouted. There really was a terrible noise
coming from somewhere. It seemed to be getting
worse every minute. Every now and then there was
a round of applause and several times he distinctly
heard the sound of people cheering.

"His *beret*," shouted Mrs. Brown in return. "A
green woollen one that came down over his ears.
With a pom-pom."

The detective shut his notebook with a snap. The
noise outside was definitely getting worse. "Pardon
me," he said, sternly. "There's something queer
going on that needs investigating."

Mrs. Brown and Judy exchanged glances. The
same thought was running through both their minds.
They both said "Paddington!" and rushed after the

detective. Mrs. Brown clung to the detective's coat and Judy clung to Mrs. Brown's as they forced their way through the crowd on the pavement. Just as they reached the window a tremendous cheer went up.

"I might have known," said Mrs. Brown.

"Paddington!" exclaimed Judy.

Paddington had just reached the top of his pyramid. At least, it had started off to be a pyramid, but it wasn't really. It wasn't any particular shape at all and it was very rickety. Having placed the last tin on the top Paddington was in trouble. He wanted to get down but he couldn't. He reached out a paw and the mountain began to wobble. Paddington clung helplessly to the tins, swaying to and fro, watched by a fascinated audience. And then, without any warning, the whole lot collapsed again, only this time Paddington was on top and not underneath. A groan of disappointment went up from the crowd.

"Best thing I've seen in years," said a man in the crowd to Mrs. Brown. "Blest if I know how they think these things up."

"Will he do it again, Mummy?" asked a small boy.

"I don't think so, dear," said his mother. "I think he's finished for the day." She pointed to the window where the detective was removing a sorry looking Paddington. Mrs. Brown hurried back to the entrance followed by Judy.

Inside the shop the detective looked at Paddington

64

and then at his notebook. " Blue duffle coat," he said.
" Green woollen beret! " He pulled the beret off.
" Black ears! I know who you are," he said grimly;
" you're Paddington! "

Paddington nearly fell over backwards with
astonishment.

" However did you know that? " he said.

" I'm a detective," said the man. " It's my job
to know these things. We're always on the look-out
for criminals."

" But I'm not a criminal," said Paddington, hotly.
" I'm a bear! Besides, I was only tidying up the
window . . ."

" Tidying up the window," the detective spluttered.
" I don't know what Mr. Perkins will have to say.
He only dressed it this morning."

Paddington looked round uneasily. He could see
Mrs. Brown and Judy hurrying towards him. In fact,
there were several people coming his way, including
an important looking man in a black coat and striped
trousers. They all reached him at the same time and
all began talking together.

Paddington sat down on his case and watched
them. There were times when it was much better
to keep quiet, and this was one of them. In the end
it was the important looking man who won, because
he had the loudest voice and kept on talking when
everyone else had finished.

To Paddington's surprise he reached down, took

hold of his paw, and started to shake it so hard he thought it was going to drop off.

"Delighted to know you, bear," he boomed. "Delighted to know you. And congratulations."

"That's all right," said Paddington, doubtfully. He didn't know why, but the man seemed very pleased.

The man turned to Mrs. Brown. "You say his name's Paddington?"

"That's right," said Mrs. Brown. "And I'm sure he didn't mean any harm."

"Harm?" The man looked at Mrs. Brown in amazement. "Did you say *harm*? My dear lady, through the action of this bear we've had the biggest crowd in years. Our telephone hasn't stopped ringing." He waved towards the entrance to the store. "And still they come!"

He placed his hand on Paddington's head. "Barkridges," he said, "Barkridges is grateful!" He waved his other hand for silence. "We should like to show our gratitude. If there is anything . . . anything in the store you would like . . .?"

Paddington's eyes gleamed. He knew just what he wanted. He'd seen it on their way up to the outfitting department. It had been standing all by itself on a counter in the food store. The biggest one he'd ever seen. Almost as big as himself.

"Please," he said, "I'd like one of those jars of marmalade. One of the big ones."

If the manager of Barkridges felt surprised he didn't show it. He stood respectfully to one side, by the entrance to the lift.

" Marmalade it shall be," he said, pressing the button.

" I think," said Paddington, " if you don't mind, I'd rather use the stairs."

CHAPTER FIVE

Paddington and the ' Old Master '

PADDINGTON SOON settled down and became one of
the family. In fact, in no time at all it was difficult
to imagine what life had been like without him. He
made himself useful about the house and the days
passed quickly. The Browns lived near the Portobello
Road where there was a big market and quite often,
when Mrs. Brown was busy, she let him go out to
do the shopping for her. Mr. Brown made a shopping
trolley for him—an old basket on wheels with a
handle for steering it.

Paddington was a good shopper and soon became

well known to all the traders in the market. He was very thorough and took the job of shopping seriously. He would press the fruit to see that it had the right degree of firmness, as Mrs. Bird had shown him, and he was always on the look-out for bargains. He was a popular bear with the traders and most of them went out of their way to save the best things of the day for him.

" That bear gets more for his shilling than anyone I know," said Mrs. Bird. " I don't know how he gets away with it, really I don't. It must be the mean streak in him."

" I'm not mean," said Paddington, indignantly. " I'm just careful, that's all."

" Whatever it is," replied Mrs. Bird, " you're worth your weight in gold."

Paddington took this remark very seriously, and spent a long time weighing himself on the bathroom scales. Eventually he decided to consult his friend, Mr. Gruber, on the subject.

Now Paddington spent a lot of his time looking in shop windows, and of all the windows in the Portobello Road, Mr. Gruber's was the best. For one thing it was nice and low so that he could look in without having to stand on tiptoe, and for another, it was full of interesting things. Old pieces of furniture, medals, pots and pans, pictures; there were so many things it was difficult to get inside the shop, and old Mr. Gruber spent a lot of his time sitting in a deckchair on the pavement. Mr. Gruber, in his turn, found Paddington very interesting and soon they had become great friends. Paddington often stopped there on his way home from a shopping expedition and they spent many hours discussing South America, where Mr. Gruber had been when he was a boy. Mr. Gruber usually had a bun and a cup of cocoa in the morning for what he called his ' elevenses,' and he had taken to sharing it with Paddington. " There's nothing like a nice chat over a bun and a cup of cocoa," he used to say, and Paddington, who liked all three, agreed with him—even though the cocoa did make his whiskers go a funny colour.

Paddington was always interested in bright things and he had consulted Mr. Gruber one morning on the subject of his Peruvian centavos. He had an idea in the back of his mind that if they were worth a lot of money he could perhaps sell them and buy a present for the Browns. The one and sixpence a week pocket-money Mr. Brown gave him was nice, but by the time he had bought some buns on a Saturday morning there wasn't much left. After a great deal of consideration, Mr. Gruber had advised Paddington to keep the coins. " It's not always the brightest things that fetch the most money, Mr. Brown," he had said. Mr. Gruber always called Paddington ' Mr. Brown,' and it made him feel very important.

He had taken Paddington into the back of the shop where his desk was, and from a drawer he had taken a cardboard box full of old coins. They had been rather dirty and disappointing. " See these, Mr. Brown ? " he had said. " These are what they call sovereigns. You wouldn't think they were very valuable to look at them, but they are. They're made of gold and they're worth seventy shillings each. That's more than ten pounds for an ounce. If you ever find any of those, just you bring them to me."

One day, having weighed himself carefully on the scales, Paddington hurried round to Mr. Gruber, taking with him a piece of paper from his scrapbook, covered with mysterious calculations. After a big meal on a Sunday, Paddington had discovered he weighed nearly sixteen pounds. That was . . . he looked at his piece of paper again as he neared Mr. Gruber's shop . . . that was nearly two hundred and sixty ounces, which meant he was worth nearly two thousand five hundred pounds!

Mr. Gruber listened carefully to all that Paddington had to tell him and then closed his eyes and thought 'for a moment. He was a kindly man, and he didn't want to disappoint Paddington.

" I've no doubt," he said, at last, " that you're *worth* that. You're obviously a very valuable young bear. I know it. Mr. and Mrs. Brown know it. Mrs. Bird knows it. But do other people ? "

He looked at Paddington over his glasses. " Things aren't always what they seem in this world, Mr. Brown," he said, sadly.

Paddington sighed. It was very disappointing. " I wish they were," he said. " It would be so nice."

" Perhaps," said Mr. Gruber, mysteriously. " Perhaps. But we shouldn't have any nice surprises then, should we? "

He took Paddington into his shop and after offering

him a seat disappeared for a moment. When he returned he was carrying a large picture of a boat. At least, half of it was a boat. The other half seemed to be the picture of a lady in a large hat.

" There you are," he said, proudly. " That's what I mean by things not always being what they seem. I'd like your opinion on it, Mr. Brown."

Paddington felt rather flattered but also puzzled.

The picture didn't seem to be one thing or the other and he said so.

"Ah," said Mr. Gruber, delightedly. "It isn't at the moment. But just you wait until I've cleaned it! I gave five shillings for that picture years and years ago, when it was just a picture of a sailing ship. And what do you think? When I started to clean it the other day all the paint began to come off and I discovered there was another painting underneath." He looked around and then lowered his voice. "Nobody else knows," he whispered, "but I think the one underneath may be valuable. It may be what they call an 'old master.'"

Seeing that Paddington still looked puzzled, he explained to him that in the old days, when artists ran short of money and couldn't afford any canvas to paint on, they sometimes painted on top of old pictures. And sometimes, very occasionally, they painted them on top of pictures by artists who afterwards became famous and whose pictures were worth a lot of money. But as they had been painted over, no one knew anything about them.

"It all sounds very complicated," said Paddington thoughtfully.

Mr. Gruber talked for a long time about painting, which was one of his favourite subjects. But Paddington, though he was usually interested in anything Mr. Gruber had to tell him, was hardly listening. Eventually, refusing Mr. Gruber's offer of a second cup of cocoa, he slipped down off the chair and began making his way home. He raised his hat automatically whenever anyone said good-day to him, but there was a far away expression in his eyes. Even the smell of buns from the bakery passed by unheeded. Paddington had an idea.

When he got home he went upstairs to his room and lay on the bed for a long while staring up at the ceiling. He was up there so long that Mrs. Bird became quite worried and poked her head round the door to know if he was all right.

"Quite all right, thank you," said Paddington, distantly. "I'm just thinking."

Mrs. Bird closed the door and hurried downstairs to tell the others. Her news had a mixed reception. "I don't mind him *just* thinking," said Mrs. Brown, with a worried expression on her face. "It's when he actually thinks *of* something that the trouble starts."

But she was in the middle of her housework and soon forgot the matter. Certainly both she and Mrs. Bird were much too busy to notice the small figure of a bear creeping cautiously in the direction of Mr. Brown's shed a few minutes later. Nor did they see him return armed with a bottle of Mr. Brown's paint remover and a large pile of rags. Had they done so they might have had good cause to worry. And if Mrs. Brown had seen him creeping on tiptoe into the drawing-room, closing the door carefully behind him, she wouldn't have had a minute's peace.

Fortunately everyone was much too busy to notice any of these things. Even more fortunately, no one came into the drawing-room for quite a long while. Because Paddington was in a mess. Things hadn't gone at all according to plan. He was beginning to wish he had listened more carefully to the things Mr. Gruber had said on the subject of cleaning paintings.

To start with, even though he'd used almost half a bottle of Mr. Brown's paint remover, the picture had only come off in patches. Secondly, and what was even worse, where it *had* come off there was nothing underneath. Only the white canvas. Paddington stood back and surveyed his handiwork. Originally it had been a painting of a lake, with a blue sky and several sailing boats dotted around. Now it looked like a storm at sea. All the boats had gone, the sky was a funny shade of grey, and half the lake had disappeared.

"What a good thing I found this old box of paints," he thought, as he stood back holding the end of the brush at paw's length and squinting at it as he'd once seen a real artist do. Holding a palette in his left paw, he squeezed some red paint on to it and then splodged it about with the brush. He looked nervously over his shoulder and then dabbed some of it on to the canvas.

Paddington had found the paints in a cupboard under the stairs. A whole box of them. There were reds and greens and yellows and blues. In fact, there were

so many different colours it was difficult to know which to choose first.

He wiped the brush carefully on his hat and tried another colour and then another. It was all so interesting that he thought he would try a bit of each, and he very soon forgot the fact that he was supposed to be painting a picture.

In fact, it was more of a design than a picture, with lines and circles and crosses all in different colours. Even Paddington was startled when he finally stepped back to examine it. Of the original picture there was no trace at all. Rather sadly he put the tubes of paint back into the box and wrapped the picture in a canvas bag, leaning it against the wall, exactly as he'd found it. He decided reluctantly to have another try later on. Painting was fun while it lasted but it was much more difficult than it looked.

He was very silent all through dinner that evening. He was so silent that several times Mrs. Brown asked him how he was, until eventually Paddington asked to be excused and went upstairs.

" I do hope he's all right, Henry," she said, after he'd gone. " He hardly touched his dinner and that's so unlike him. And he seemed to have some funny red spots all over his face."

" Crikey," said Jonathan. " Red spots! I hope he's given it to me, whatever it is, then I shan't have to go back to school! "

"Well, he's got green ones as well," said Judy.
"I saw some green ones!"

"*Green* ones!" Even Mr. Brown looked worried.
"I wonder if he's sickening for anything? If
they're not gone in the morning I'll send for the
doctor."

"He was so looking forward to going to the
handicrafts exhibition, too," said Mrs. Brown. "It'll
be a shame if he has to stay in bed."

"Do you think you'll win a prize with your
painting, Dad?" asked Jonathan.

"No one will be more surprised than your father
if he does," replied Mrs. Brown. "He's never won
a prize yet!"

"What is it, Daddy?" asked Judy. "Aren't you
going to tell us?"

"It's meant to be a surprise," said Mr. Brown
modestly. "It took me a long time to do. It's
painted from memory."

Painting was one of Mr. Brown's hobbies, and once
a year he entered a picture for a handicrafts exhibition
which was held in Kensington, near where they lived.
Several famous people came to judge the pictures and
there were a number of prizes. There were also lots
of other competitions, and it was a sore point with
Mr. Brown that he had never won anything, whereas
twice Mrs. Brown had won a prize in the rug-making
competition.

"Anyway," he said, declaring the subject closed,

" it's too late now. The man collected it this afternoon, so we shall see what we shall see."

The sun was shining the next day and the exhibition was crowded. Everyone was pleased that Paddington looked so much better. His spots had completely disappeared and he ate a large breakfast to make up for missing so much dinner the night before. Only Mrs. Bird had her suspicions when she found Paddington's ' spots ' on his towel in the bathroom, but she kept her thoughts to herself.

The Browns occupied the middle five seats of the front row where the judging was to take place. There was an air of great excitement. It was news to Paddington that Mr. Brown actually painted and he was looking forward to seeing a picture by someone he knew.

On the platform several important looking men with beards were bustling about talking to each other and waving their arms in the air. They appeared to be having a great deal of argument about one painting in particular.

" Henry," whispered Mrs. Brown, excitedly. " I do believe they're talking about yours. I recognise the canvas bag."

Mr. Brown looked puzzled. " It certainly looks like my bag," he said. " But I don't think it can be. All the canvas was stuck to the painting. Didn't you see? Just as if someone had put it inside while it was still wet. I painted mine ages ago."

79

Paddington sat very still and stared straight ahead, hardly daring to move. He had a strange sinking feeling in the bottom of his stomach, as if something awful was about to happen. He began to wish he hadn't washed his spots off that morning; then at least he could have stayed in bed.

Judy poked him with her elbow. " What's the matter, Paddington? " she asked. " You look most peculiar. Are you all right? "

" I don't feel ill," said Paddington in a small voice. " But I think I'm in trouble again."

" Oh dear," said Judy. " Well, keep your paws crossed. This is it! "

Paddington sat up. One of the men on the platform, the most important looking one with the biggest beard, was speaking. And there . . . Paddington's knees began to tremble . . . there, on the platform, on an easel in full view of everyone, was ' his ' picture!

He was so dazed he only caught scraps of what the man was saying.

" . . . remarkable use of colour . . ."

" . . . very unusual . . ."

" . . . great imagination . . . a credit to the artist . . ."

And then, he almost fell off his seat with surprise. " The winner of the first prize is Mr. Henry Brown of thirty-two Windsor Gardens! "

Paddington wasn't the only one who felt surprised. Mr. Brown, who was being helped up on to the platform, looked as if he had just been struck by lightning. " But . . . but . . ." he stuttered, " there must be some mistake."

" Mistake? " said the man with the beard. " Non-sense, my dear sir. Your name's on the back of the canvas. You *are* Mr. Brown, aren't you? Mr. *Henry* Brown? "

Mr. Brown looked at the painting with unbelieving eyes. " It's certainly my name on the back," he said. " It's my writing . . ." He left the sentence unfinished and looked down towards the audience. He had his own ideas on the subject, but it was difficult to catch Paddington's eye. It usually was when you particularly wanted to.

" I think," said Mr. Brown, when the applause had died down, and he had accepted the cheque for ten pounds which the man gave him, " proud as I am,

I think I would like to donate the prize to a certain home for retired bears in South America." A murmur of surprise went round the assembly but it passed over Paddington's head, though he would have been very pleased had he known its cause. He was staring hard at the painting, and in particular at the man with the large beard, who was beginning to look hot and bothered.

" I think," said Paddington, to the world in general, " they might have stood it the right way up. It's not every day a bear wins first prize in a painting competition! "

CHAPTER SIX

A Visit to the Theatre

THE BROWNS were all very excited. Mr. Brown had been given tickets for a box at the theatre. It was the first night of a brand new play, and the leading part was being played by the world famous actor, Sir Sealy Bloom. Even Paddington became infected with the excitement. He made several journeys to his friend, Mr. Gruber, to have the theatre explained to him. Mr. Gruber thought he was very lucky to be going to the first night of a new play. " All sorts of famous people will be there," he said. " I don't suppose many bears have that sort of opportunity once in a lifetime."

Mr. Gruber lent Paddington several second-hand

books about the theatre. He was rather a slow reader but there were lots of pictures, and in one of them, a big cut-out model of a stage which sprang up every time he opened the pages. Paddington decided that when he grew up he wanted to be an actor. He took to standing on his dressing-table and striking poses in the mirror just as he had seen them in the books.

Mrs. Brown had her own thoughts on the subject. "I *do* hope it's a nice play," she said to Mrs. Bird. "You know what Paddington's like . . . he does take these things so seriously."

"Oh, well," said Mrs. Bird, "*I* shall sit at home and listen to the wireless in peace and quiet. But it'll be an experience for him and he does like experiences so. Besides, he's been very good lately."

"I know," said Mrs. Brown. "That's what worries me!"

As it turned out, the play itself was the least of Mrs. Brown's worries. Paddington was unusually silent all the way to the theatre. It was the first time he had been out after dark and the very first time he had seen the lights of London. Mr. Brown pointed out all the famous landmarks as they drove past in the car, and it was a gay party of Browns that eventually trooped into the theatre.

Paddington was pleased to find it all exactly as Mr. Gruber had described it to him, even down to the commissionaire who opened the door for them and saluted as they entered the foyer.

Paddington returned the salute with a wave of his paw and then sniffed. Everything was painted red and gold and the theatre had a nice, warm, friendly sort of smell. There was a slight upset at the cloakroom when he found he had to pay sixpence in order to leave his duffle coat and suitcase. The woman behind the counter turned quite nasty when Paddington asked for his things back.

She was still talking about it in a loud voice as the attendant led them along a passage towards their seats. At the entrance to the box the attendant paused.

" Programme, sir? " she said to Paddington.

" Yes, please," said Paddington, taking five. " Thank you very much."

" And would you like coffee in the interval, sir? " she asked.

Paddington's eyes glistened. " Oh yes, please," he said, imagining it was a kind thought on the part of the theatre. He tried to push his way past, but the attendant barred the way.

" That'll be twelve and sixpence," she said. " Sixpence each for the programmes and two shillings each for the coffee."

Paddington looked as if he could hardly believe his ears. " Twelve shillings and sixpence? " he repeated. " *Twelve shillings and sixpence?* "

" That's all right, Paddington," said Mr. Brown, anxious to avoid another fuss. " It's my treat. You go in and sit down."

85

Paddington obeyed like a shot, but he gave the attendant some very queer looks while she arranged some cushions for his seat in the front row. All the same, he was pleased to see she had given him the one nearest the stage. He'd already sent a postcard to his Aunt Lucy with a carefully drawn copy of a plan of the theatre, which he'd found in one of Mr. Gruber's books, and a small cross in one corner marked 'MY SEET.'

The theatre was quite full and Paddington waved to the people down below. Much to Mrs. Brown's embarrassment, several of them pointed and waved back.

" I *do* wish he wouldn't be quite so friendly," she whispered to Mr. Brown.

" Wouldn't you like to take off your duffle coat now ? " asked Mr. Brown. " It'll be cold when you go out again."

Paddington climbed up and stood on his chair. " I think perhaps I will," he said. " It's getting warm."

Judy started to help him off with it. " Mind my marmalade sandwich! " cried Paddington, as she placed it on the ledge in front of him. But it was too late. He looked round guiltily.

" Crikey! " said Jonathan. " It's fallen on some-one's head! " He looked over the edge of the box. " It's that man with the bald head. He looks jolly cross."

86

"Oh, Paddington!" Mrs. Brown looked despairingly at him. "Do you *have* to bring marmalade sandwiches to the theatre?"

"It's all right," said Paddington, cheerfully. "I've some more in the other pocket if anyone wants one. They're a bit squashed, I'm afraid, because I sat on them in the car."

"There seems to be some sort of a row going on down below," said Mr. Brown, craning his head to look over the edge. "Some chap just waved his fist at me. And what's all this about marmalade sandwiches?" Mr. Brown was a bit slow on the uptake sometimes.

"Nothing, dear," said Mrs. Brown, hastily. She

decided to let the matter drop. It was much easier in the long run.

In any case, Paddington was having a great struggle with himself over some opera glasses. He had just seen a little box in front of him marked OPERA GLASSES. SIXPENCE. Eventually, after a great deal of thought, he unlocked his suitcase and from a secret compartment withdrew a sixpence.

" I don't think much of these," he said, a moment later, looking through them at the audience. " Everyone looks smaller."

" You've got them the wrong way round, silly," said Jonathan.

" Well, I still don't think much of them," said Paddington, turning them round. " I wouldn't have bought them if I'd known. Still," he added, after a moment's thought. " They might come in useful next time."

Just as he began to speak the overture came to an end and the curtain rose. The scene was the living room of a large house, and Sir Sealy Bloom, in the part of a village squire, was pacing up and down. There was a round of applause from the audience.

" You don't take them home," whispered Judy. " You have to put them back when you leave."

" WHAT! " cried Paddington, in a loud voice. Several calls of ' hush ' came from the darkened theatre as Sir Sealy Bloom paused and looked pointedly

in the direction of the Browns' box. " Do you mean
to say . . ." words failed Paddington for the moment.
" *Sixpence!* " he said, bitterly. " That's three buns'
worth! " He turned his gaze on Sir Sealy Bloom.

Sir Sealy Bloom looked rather irritable. He didn't
like first nights, and this one in particular had started
badly. He had a nasty feeling about it. He much
preferred playing the hero, where he had the sympathy
of the audience, and in this play he was the villain.
Being the first night of the play, he wasn't at all sure
of some of his lines. To make matters worse, he had
arrived at the theatre only to discover that the prompt
boy was missing and there was no one else to take his
place. Then there was the disturbance in the stalls
just before the curtain went up. Something to do
with a marmalade sandwich, so the stage manager
had said. Of course, that was all nonsense, but still,
it was very disturbing. And then there was this noisy
crowd in the box. He sighed to himself. It was
obviously going to be one of those nights.

But if Sir Sealy Bloom's heart was not in the play,
Paddington's certainly was. He soon forgot about
his wasted sixpence and devoted all his attention to
the plot. He decided quite early on that he didn't
like Sir Sealy Bloom and he stared at him hard
through his opera glasses. He followed his every
move and when, at the end of the first act, Sir Sealy,
in the part of the hard-hearted father, turned his
daughter out into the world without a penny, Pad-

dington stood up on his chair and waved his pro-gramme indignantly at the stage.

Paddington was a surprising bear in many ways and he had a strong sense of right and wrong. As the curtain came down he placed his opera glasses firmly on the ledge and climbed off his seat.

" Are you enjoying it, Paddington? " asked Mr. Brown.

" It's very interesting," said Paddington. He had a determined note to his voice and Mrs. Brown looked at him sharply. She was beginning to recognise that tone and it worried her.

" Where are you going, dear? " she asked, as he made for the door of the box.

" Oh, just out for a walk," said Paddington, vaguely.

" Well, don't be too long," she called, as the door closed behind him. " You don't want to miss any of the second act."

" Oh, don't fuss, Mary," said Mr. Brown. " I expect he just wants to stretch his legs or something. He's probably gone out to the cloakroom."

But at that moment Paddington was going, not in the direction of the cloakroom, but towards a door leading to the back of the theatre. It was marked PRIVATE. ARTISTS ONLY. As he pushed the door open and passed through, he immediately found himself in an entirely different world. There were no red plush seats; everything was very bare. Lots of ropes hung down from the roof, pieces of scenery were stacked against the walls, and everyone seemed in a great hurry. Normally Paddington would have been most interested in everything, but now he had a purposeful look on his face.

Seeing a man bending over some scenery, he walked over and tapped him on the shoulder. " Excuse me," he said. " Can you tell me where the man is? "

The scene hand went on working. " Man? " he said. " *What* man? "

" *The* man," said Paddington, patiently. " The nasty man."

" Oh, you mean Sir Sealy." The scene hand pointed towards a long corridor. " He's in his dressing-room. You'd better not go disturbing him 'cause he's not in a very good mood." He looked up. " Hey! " he cried. " You're not supposed to be in here. Who let you in? "

Paddington was too far away to answer even if he had heard. He was already half-way up the corridor, looking closely at all the doors. Eventually he came to one with a large star on it and the words SIR SEALY BLOOM in big gold letters. Paddington drew a deep breath and then knocked loudly. There was no reply, so he knocked again. Still there was no reply, and so, very cautiously, he pushed open the door with his paw.

" Go away! " said a booming voice. " I don't want to see anyone."

91

Paddington peered round the door. Sir Sealy Bloom was lying stretched out on a long couch. He looked tired and cross. He opened one eye and gazed at Paddington.

" I'm not signing any autographs," he growled.

" I don't want your autograph," said Paddington, fixing him with a hard stare. " I wouldn't want your autograph if I had my autograph book, and I haven't got my autograph book so there! "

Sir Sealy sat up. " You don't want my autograph? " he said, in a surprised voice. " But everyone always wants my autograph! "

" Well, I don't," said Paddington. " I've come to tell you to take your daughter back! " He gulped the last few words. The great man seemed to have grown to about twice the size he had been on the stage, and he looked as if he was going to explode at any minute.

Sir Sealy clutched his forehead. " You want me to take my daughter back? " he said at last.

" That's right," said Paddington, firmly. " And if you don't, I expect she can come and stay with Mr. and Mrs. Brown."

Sir Sealy Bloom ran his hand distractedly through his hair and then pinched himself. " Mr. and Mrs. *Brown*," he repeated in a dazed voice. He looked wildly round the room and then dashed to the door. " Sarah! " he called, in a loud voice. " Sarah, come in here at once! " He backed round the room until he had placed the couch between himself and Paddington. " Keep away, bear! " he said, dramatically, and then peered at Paddington, for he was rather short-sighted. " You *are* a bear, aren't you? " he added.

" That's right," said Paddington. " From Darkest Peru! "

Sir Sealy looked at his woollen hat. " Well then," he said crossly, playing for time, " you ought to know better than to wear a green hat in my dressing-room. Don't you know green is a very unlucky colour in the theatre? Take it off at once."

" It's not my fault," said Paddington. " I wanted to wear my proper hat." He had just started to explain all about his hat when the door burst open and the lady called Sarah entered. Paddington immediately recognised her as Sir Sealy's daughter in the play.

" It's all right," he said. " I've come to rescue you."

" You've *what?* " The lady seemed most surprised.

" Sarah," Sir Sealy Bloom came out from behind the couch. " Sarah, protect me from this . . . this mad bear! "

" I'm not mad," said Paddington, indignantly.

" Then kindly explain what you are doing in my dressing-room," boomed the great actor.

Paddington sighed. Sometimes people were very slow to understand things. Patiently he explained it

93

all to them. When he had finished, the lady called Sarah threw back her head and laughed.

" I'm glad you think it's funny," said Sir Sealy.

" But darling, don't you see? " she said. " It's a great compliment. Paddington really believes you were throwing me out into the world without a penny. It shows what a great actor you are! "

Sir Sealy thought for a moment. " Humph! " he said, gruffly. " Quite an understandable mistake, I suppose. He looks a remarkably intelligent bear, come to think of it."

Paddington looked from one to the other. " Then you were only acting all the time," he faltered.

The lady bent down and took his paw. " Of course, darling. But it was very kind of you to come to my rescue. I shall always remember it."

" Well, I *would* have rescued you if you'd wanted it," said Paddington.

Sir Sealy coughed. " Are you interested in the theatre, bear? " he boomed.

" Oh, yes," said Paddington. " *Very* much. Except I don't like having to pay sixpence for everything. I want to be an actor when I grow up."

The lady called Sarah jumped up. " Why, Sealy darling," she said, looking at Paddington. " I've an idea! " She whispered in Sir Sealy's ear and then Sir Sealy looked at Paddington. " It's a bit unusual," he said, thoughtfully. " But it's worth a try. Yes, it's certainly worth a try! "

In the theatre itself the interval was almost at an end and the Browns were getting restless.

" Oh, dear," said Mrs. Brown. " I wonder where he's got to? "

" If he doesn't hurry up," said Mr. Brown, " he's going to miss the start of the second act."

Just then there was a knock at the door and an attendant handed a note to Mr. Brown. " A young bear gentleman asked me to give you this," he announced. " He said it was very urgent."

" Er . . . thank you," said Mr. Brown, taking the note and opening it.

" What does it say? " asked Mrs. Brown, anxiously. " Is he all right? "

Mr. Brown handed her the note to read. " Your guess is as good as mine," he said.

Mrs. Brown looked at it. It was hastily written in pencil and it said: I HAVE BEEN GIVEN A VERRY IMPORT-ANT JOB. PADINGTUN. P.S. I WILL TEL YOU ABOUT IT LAYTER.

" Now what on earth can that mean? " said Mrs. Brown. " Trust something unusual to happen to Paddington."

" I don't know," said Mr. Brown, settling back in his chair as the lights went down. " But I'm not going to let it spoil the play."

" I hope the second half is better than the first," said Jonathan. " I thought the first half was rotten. That man kept on forgetting his lines."

95

The second half *was* much better than the first. From the moment Sir Sealy strode on to the stage the theatre was electrified. A great change had come over him. He no longer fumbled over his lines, and people who had coughed all through the first half now sat up in their seats and hung on his every word.

When the curtain finally came down on the end of the play, with Sir Sealy's daughter returning to his arms, there was a great burst of applause. The curtain rose again and the whole company bowed to the audience. Then it rose while Sir Sealy and Sarah bowed, but still the cheering went on. Finally Sir Sealy stepped forward and raised his hand for quiet.

"Ladies and gentlemen," he said. "Thank you for your kind applause. We are indeed most grateful. But before you leave I would like to introduce the youngest and most important member of our company. A young . . . er, bear, who came to our rescue . . ." The rest of Sir Sealy's speech was drowned in a buzz of excitement as he stepped forward to the very front of the stage, where a small screen hid a hole in the boards which was the prompt box.

He took hold of one of Paddington's paws and pulled. Paddington's head appeared through the hole. In his other paw he was grasping a copy of the script.

"Come along, Paddington," said Sir Sealy. "Come and take your bow."

96

" I can't," gasped Paddington. " I think I'm stuck! "

And stuck he was. It took several stagehands, the fireman, and a lot of butter to remove him after the audience had gone. But he was far enough out to twist round and raise his hat to the cheering crowd before the curtain came down for the last time.

Several nights later, anyone going into Paddington's room would have found him sitting up in bed with his scrapbook, a pair of scissors, and a pot of paste. He was busy pasting in a picture of Sir Sealy Bloom, which the great man had signed: ' To Paddington, with grateful thanks.' There was also a signed picture from the lady called Sarah, and one of his proudest possessions—a newspaper cutting about the play headed PADDINGTON SAVES THE DAY!

Mr. Gruber had told him that the photographs were probably worth a bit of money, but after much thought he had decided not to part with them. In any case, Sir Sealy Bloom had given him his sixpence back *and* a pair of opera glasses.

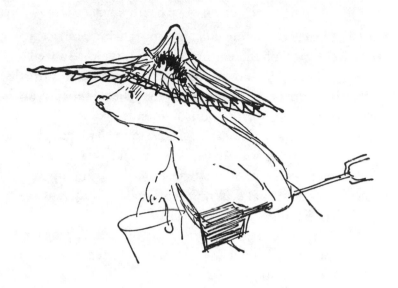

CHAPTER SEVEN

Adventure at the Seaside

ONE MORNING Mr. Brown tapped the barometer in
the hall. " It looks as if it's going to be a nice day,"
he said. " How about a trip to the sea? "

His remark was greeted with enthusiasm by the
rest of the family, and in no time at all the house was
in an uproar.

Mrs. Bird started to cut a huge pile of sandwiches
while Mr. Brown got the car ready. Jonathan and
Judy searched for their bathing suits and Paddington
went up to his room to pack. An outing which
involved Paddington was always rather a business,

as he insisted on taking all his things with him. As
time went by he had acquired lots of things. As well
as his suitcase, he now had a smart week-end grip
with the initials P.B. inscribed on the side and a
paper carrier-bag for the odds and ends.

For the summer months Mrs. Brown had bought
him a sun hat. It was made of straw and very floppy.
Paddington liked it, for by turning the brim up or
down, he could make it different shapes, and it was
really like having several hats in one.

" When we get to Brightsea," said Mrs. Brown,
" we'll buy you a bucket and spade. Then you can
make a sand-castle."

" And you can go on the pier," said Jonathan,
eagerly. " They've some super machines on the pier.
You'd better bring plenty of pennies."

" And we can go swimming," added Judy. " You
can swim, can't you? "

" Not very well, I'm afraid," replied Paddington.
" You see, I've never been to the seaside before! "

" *Never* been to the seaside! " Everyone stopped
what they were doing and stared at Paddington.

" Never," said Paddington.

They all agreed that it must be nice to be going to
the seaside for the first time in one's life; even Mrs.
Bird began talking about the time she first went to
Brightsea, many years before. Paddington became
very excited as they told him all about the wonderful
things he was going to see.

The car was crowded when they started off. Mrs. Bird, Judy and Jonathan sat in the back. Mr. Brown drove and Mrs. Brown and Paddington sat beside him. Paddington liked sitting in the front, especially when the window was open, so that he could poke his head out in the cool breeze. After a minor delay when Paddington's hat blew off on the outskirts of London, they were soon on the open road.

" Can you smell the sea yet, Paddington? " asked Mrs. Brown after a while.

Paddington poked his head out and sniffed. " I can smell something," he said.

"Well," said Mr. Brown. " Keep on sniffing, because we're almost there." And sure enough, as they reached the top of a hill and rounded a corner to go down the other side, there it was in the distance, glistening in the morning sun.

Paddington's eyes opened wide. " Look at all the boats on the dirt! " he cried, pointing in the direction of the beach with his paw.

Everyone laughed. " That's not dirt," said Judy. " That's sand." By the time they had explained all about sand to Paddington they were in Brightsea itself, and driving along the front. Paddington looked at the sea rather doubtfully. The waves were much bigger than he had imagined. Not so big as the ones he'd seen on his journey to England, but quite large enough for a small bear.

Mr. Brown stopped the car by a shop on the

esplanade and took out some money. " I'd like to fit this bear out for a day at the seaside," he said to the lady behind the counter. " Let's see now, we shall need a bucket and spade, a pair of sun-glasses, one of those rubber tyres . . ." As he reeled off the list, the lady handed the articles to Paddington, who began to wish he had more than two paws. He had a rubber tyre round his middle which kept slipping down around his knees, a pair of sun-glasses balanced precariously on his nose, his straw hat, a bucket and spade in one hand, and his suitcase in the other.

" Photograph, sir? " Paddington turned to see an untidy man with a camera looking at him. " Only a shilling, sir. Results guaranteed. Money back if you're not satisfied."

Paddington considered the matter for a moment. He didn't like the look of the man very much, but he had been saving hard for several weeks and now had just over three shillings. It would be nice to have a picture of himself.

" Won't take a minute, sir," said the man, disappearing behind a black cloth at the back of the camera. " Just watch the birdie."

Paddington looked around. There was no bird in sight as far as he could see. He went round behind the man and tapped him. The photographer, who appeared to be looking for something, jumped and then emerged from under his cloth. " How do you expect me to take your picture if you don't stand in front?" he asked in an aggrieved voice. "Now I've wasted a plate, and "—he looked shiftily at Paddington —"that will cost you a shilling!"

Paddington gave him a hard stare. "You said there was a bird," he said. "And there wasn't."

"I expect it flew away when it saw your face," said the man nastily. "Now where's my shilling?"

Paddington looked at him even harder for a moment. "Perhaps the bird took it when it flew away," he said.

"Ha! Ha! Ha!" cried another photographer, who had been watching the proceedings with interest. "Fancy you being taken in by a bear, Charlie! Serves you right for trying to take photographs without a licence. Now be off with you before I call a policeman."

He watched while the other man gathered up his belongings and slouched off in the direction of the pier, then he turned to Paddington. "These people are a nuisance," he said. "Taking away the living from honest folk. You did quite right not to pay him any money. And if you'll allow me, I'd like to take a nice picture of you myself, as a reward!"

The Brown family exchanged glances. "I don't know," said Mrs. Brown. "Paddington always seems to fall on his feet."

"That's because he's a bear," said Mrs. Bird, darkly. "Bears always fall on their feet." She led the way on to the beach and carefully laid out a travelling rug on the sand behind a breakwater. "This will be as good a spot as any," she said.

" Then we shall all know where to come back to, and no one will get lost."

" The tide's out," said Mr. Brown. " So it will be nice and safe for bathing." He turned to Paddington. " Are you going in, Paddington? " he asked.

Paddington looked at the sea. " I might go for a paddle," he said.

" Well, hurry up," called Judy. " And bring your bucket and spade, then we can practise making sand-castles."

" Gosh! " Jonathan pointed to a notice pinned on the wall behind them. " Look . . . there's a sand-castle competition. Whizzo! First prize two pounds for the biggest sand-castle! "

" Suppose we all join in and make one," said Judy. " I bet the three of us together could make the biggest one you've ever seen."

"I don't think you're allowed to," said Mrs. Brown, reading the notice. "It says here everyone has to make their own."

Judy looked disappointed. "Well, I shall have a go, anyway. Come on, you two, let's have a bathe first, then we can start digging after lunch." She raced down the sand closely followed by Jonathan and Paddington. At least, Jonathan followed but Paddington only got a few yards before his lifebelt slipped down and he went headlong in the sand.

"Paddington, *do* give me your suitcase," called Mrs. Brown. "You can't take it in the sea with you. It'll get wet and be ruined."

Looking rather crestfallen, Paddington handed his things to Mrs. Brown for safekeeping and then ran down the beach after the others. Judy and Jonathan were already a long way out when he got there, so he contented himself with sitting on the water's edge

for a while, letting the waves swirl around him as
they came in. It was a nice feeling, a bit cold at first,
but he soon got warm. He decided the seaside was a
nice place to be. He paddled out to where the water
was deeper and then lay back in his rubber tyre,
letting the waves carry him gently back to the shore.

"Two pounds! Supposing . . . supposing he won
two whole pounds!" He closed his eyes. In his
mind he had a picture of a beautiful castle made of
sand, like the one he'd once seen in a picture-book,
with battlements and towers and a moat. It was
getting bigger and bigger and everyone else on the
beach had stopped to gather round and cheer. Several
people said they had never seen such a big sand-castle,
and . . . he woke with a start as he felt someone
splashing water on him.

"Come on, Paddington," said Judy. "Lying there
in the sun fast asleep. It's time for lunch, and we've
got lots of work to do afterwards." Paddington felt
disappointed. It had been a nice sand-castle in his

dream. He was sure it would have won first prize. He rubbed his eyes and followed Judy and Jonathan up the beach to where Mrs. Bird had laid out the sandwiches—ham, egg and cheese for every one else, and special marmalade ones for Paddington—with ice-cream and fruit salad to follow.

" I vote," said Mr. Brown, who had in mind an after-lunch nap for himself, " that after we've eaten, you all go off in different directions and make your own sand-castles. Then we'll have our own private competition as well as the official one. I'll give two shillings to the one with the biggest castle."

All three thought this was a good idea. " But don't go too far away," called Mrs. Brown, as Jonathan, Judy and Paddington set off. " Remember the tide's coming in!" Her advice fell on deaf ears; they were all much too interested in sand-castles. Paddington especially was gripping his bucket and spade in a very determined fashion.

The beach was crowded and he had to walk quite a long way before he found a deserted spot. First of all he dug a big moat in a circle, leaving himself a drawbridge so that he could fetch and carry the sand for the castle itself. Then he set to work carrying bucketloads of sand to build the walls of the castle.

He was an industrious bear and even though it was hard work and his legs and paws soon got tired, he persevered until he had a huge pile of sand in the middle of his circle. Then he set to work with his spade, smoothing out the walls and making the battlements. They were very good battlements, with holes for windows and slots for the archers to fire through.

When he had finished he stuck his spade in one of the corner towers, placed his hat on top of that, and then lay down inside next to his marmalade jar and closed his eyes. He felt tired, but very pleased with himself. With the gentle roar of the sea in his ears he soon went fast asleep.

" We've been all along the beach," said Jonathan. " And we can't see him anywhere."

" He didn't even have his life-belt with him," said Mrs. Brown anxiously. " Nothing. Just a bucket and spade." The Browns were gathered in a worried group round the man from the lifesaving hut.

" He's been gone several hours," said Mr. Brown. " And the tide's been in over two! "

The man looked serious. " And you say he can't swim? " he asked.

" He doesn't even like having a bath much," said Judy. " So I'm sure he can't swim."

" Here's his photograph," said Mrs. Bird. " He only had it taken this morning." She handed the man Paddington's picture and then dabbed at her eyes with a handkerchief. " I know something's happened to him. He wouldn't have missed tea unless something was wrong."

The man looked at the picture. "We *could* send out a description," he said, dubiously. "But it's a job to see what he looks like by that. It's all hat and dark glasses."

"Can't you launch a lifeboat?" asked Jonathan, hopefully.

"We could," said the man. "If we knew where to look. But he might be anywhere."

"Oh, dear," Mrs. Brown reached for her handkerchief as well. "I can't bear to think about it."

"Something will turn up," said Mrs. Bird, comfortingly. "He's got a good head on his shoulders."

"Well," said the man, holding up a dripping straw hat. "You'd better have this, and in the meantime . . . we'll see what we can do."

"There, there, Mary!" Mr. Brown held his wife's arm. "Perhaps he just left it on the beach or something. It may have got picked up by the tide." He bent down to pick up the rest of Paddington's belongings. They seemed very small and lonely, lying there on their own.

"It's Paddington's hat all right," said Judy, examining it. "Look—it's got his mark inside!" She turned the hat inside out and showed them the outline of a paw mark in black ink and the words MY HAT—PADINGTUN.

"I vote we all separate," said Jonathan, "and comb the beach. We'll stand more chance that way."

Mr. Brown looked dubious. " It's getting dark," he said.

Mrs. Bird put down the travelling rug and folded her arms. " Well, I'm not going back until he's found," she said. " I couldn't go back to that empty house—not without Paddington."

" No one's thinking of going back without him, Mrs. Bird," said Mr. Brown. He looked helplessly out to sea. " It's just . . ."

" P'raps he didn't get swep' out to sea," said the lifesaving man, helpfully. " P'raps he's just gone on the pier or something. There seems to be a big crowd heading that way. Must be something interesting going on." He called out to a man who was just passing. " What's going on at the pier, chum? "

Without stopping the man looked back over his shoulder and shouted, " Chap just crossed the Atlantic all by 'isself on a raft. 'Undreds of days without food or water so they say! " He hurried on.

The lifesaving man looked disappointed. " Another of these publicity stunts," he said. " We get 'em every year."

Mr. Brown looked thoughtful. " I wonder," he said, looking in the direction of the pier.

" It would be just like him," said Mrs. Bird. " It's the sort of thing that would happen to Paddington."

" It's got to be! " cried Jonathan. " It's just got to be! "

They all looked at each other and then, picking up

their belongings, joined the crowd hurrying in the direction of the pier. It took them a long time to force their way through the turnstile, for the news that 'something was happening on the pier' had spread and there was a great throng at the entrance. But eventually, after Mr. Brown had spoken to a policeman, a way was made for them and they were escorted to the very end, where the paddle-steamers normally tied up.

A strange sight met their eyes. Paddington, who had just been pulled out of the water by a fisherman, was sitting on his upturned bucket talking to some reporters. Several of them were taking photographs while the rest fired questions at him.

"Have you come all the way from America?" asked one reporter.

The Browns, hardly knowing whether to laugh or cry, waited eagerly for Paddington's reply.

"Well, no," said Paddington, truthfully, after a moment's pause. "Not America. But I've come a long way." He waved a paw vaguely in the direction of the sea. "I got caught by the tide, you know."

"And you sat in that bucket all the time?" asked another man, taking a picture.

"That's right," replied Paddington. "And I used my spade as a paddle. It was lucky I had it with me."

"Did you live on plankton?" queried another voice.

Paddington looked puzzled. "No," he said. "Marmalade."

Mr. Brown pushed his way through the crowd. Paddington jumped up and looked rather guilty.

" Now then," said Mr. Brown, taking his paw. " That's enough questions for to-day. This bear's been at sea for a long time and he's tired. In fact," he looked meaningly at Paddington. " He's been at sea all the afternoon! "

" Is it still only Tuesday? " asked Paddington, innocently. " I thought it was much later than that! "

" Tuesday," said Mr. Brown, firmly. " And we've been worried to death over you! "

Paddington picked up his bucket and spade and jar of marmalade. " Well," he said. " I bet not many bears have gone to sea in a bucket, all the same."

It was dark when they drove along Brightsea front on their way home. The promenade was festooned with coloured lights and even the fountains in the gardens kept changing colour. It all looked very pretty. But Paddington, who was lying in the back of the car wrapped in a blanket, was thinking of his sand-castle.

" I bet mine was bigger than anyone else's," he said, sleepily.

" Bet you mine was the biggest," said Jonathan.

" I think," said Mr. Brown, hastily, " you'd all better have two shillings just to make sure."

" Perhaps we can come again another day," said

Mrs. Brown. " Then we can have another competition. How about that, Paddington?"

There was no reply from the back of the car.
Sand-castles, paddling his bucket all across the harbour,
and the sea air had proved too much for Paddington.
He was fast asleep.

CHAPTER EIGHT

A Disappearing Trick

"Oooh," said Paddington, "is it really for me?"
He stared hungrily at the cake. It really was a
wonderful cake. One of Mrs. Bird's best. It was
covered with sugar icing and it had a cream and
marmalade filling. On the top there was one candle
and the words: TO PADDINGTON. WITH BEST WISHES
FOR A HAPPY BIRTHDAY—FROM EVERYONE.

It had been Mrs. Bird's idea to have a birthday
party. Paddington had been with them for two
months. No one, not even Paddington, knew quite

how old he was, so they decided to start again and call him one. Paddington thought this was a good idea, especially when he was told that bears had two birthdays every year—one in the summer and one in the winter.

" Just like the Queen," said Mrs. Bird. " So you ought to consider yourself very important."

Paddington did. In fact, he went round to Mr. Gruber straight away and told him the good news. Mr. Gruber looked impressed and was pleased when Paddington invited him to the party.

" It's not often anyone invites me out, Mr. Brown," he said. " I don't know when I went out last and I shall look forward to it very much indeed."

He didn't say any more at the time, but the next morning a van drew up outside the Browns' house and delivered a mysterious looking parcel from all the shopkeepers in the Portobello Market.

" Aren't you a lucky bear," exclaimed Mrs. Brown, when they opened the parcel and saw what was inside. It was a nice new shopping basket on wheels, with a bell on the side that Paddington could ring to let people know he was coming.

Paddington scratched his head. " It's a job to know what to do first," he said, as he carefully placed the basket with the other presents. " I shall have a lot of ' thank you ' letters to write."

" Perhaps you'd better leave them until to-morrow,"

said Mrs. Brown hastily. Whenever Paddington wrote any letters he generally managed to get more ink on himself than on the paper, and he was looking so unusually smart, having had a bath the night before, that it seemed a pity to spoil it.

Paddington looked disappointed. He liked writing letters. " Perhaps I can help Mrs. Bird in the kitchen," he said, hopefully.

" I'm glad to say," said Mrs. Bird, as she emerged from the kitchen, " that I've just finished. But you can lick the spoon if you like." She had bitter memories of other occasions when Paddington had ' helped ' in the kitchen. " But not too much," she warned, " or you won't have room for this."

It was then that Paddington saw his cake for the first time. His eyes, usually large and round, became so much larger and rounder, that even Mrs. Bird blushed with pride. " Special occasions demand special things," she said, and hurried off in the direction of the dining-room.

Paddington spent the rest of the day being hurried from one part of the house to another as preparations were made for his party. Mrs. Brown was busy tidying up. Mrs. Bird was busy in the kitchen. Jonathan and Judy were busy with the decorations. Everyone had a job except Paddington.

" I thought it was supposed to be *my* birthday," he grumbled, as he was sent packing into the drawing-room for the fifth time after upsetting a box of marbles over the kitchen floor.

"So it is, dear," said a flustered Mrs. Brown. "But your time comes later." She was beginning to regret telling him that bears had two birthdays every year, for already he was worrying about when the next one was due.

"Now just you watch out of the window for the postman," she said, lifting him up on to the window sill. But Paddington didn't seem very keen on this. "Or else," she said, "practise doing some of your conjuring tricks, ready for this evening."

Among Paddington's many presents was a conjuring outfit from Mr. and Mrs. Brown. It was a very expensive one from Barkridges. It had a special magic table, a large mystery box which made things disappear if you followed the instructions properly, a magic wand and several packs of cards. Paddington emptied them all over the floor and settled down in the middle to read the book of instructions.

He sat there for a long time, studying the pictures and diagrams, and reading everything twice to make sure. Every now and then he absent-mindedly dipped a paw into his marmalade pot, and then, remembering it was his birthday and that there was a big tea to come, he reached up and stood the jar on the magic table before returning to his studies.

The first chapter was called SPELLS. It showed

how to wave the magic wand and the correct way to say ABRACADABRA. Paddington stood up, clutching the book in one paw, and waved the wand several times through the air. He also tried saying ABRACADABRA. He looked around. Nothing seemed to have changed, and he was just about to try again, when his eyes nearly popped out of his head. The jar of marmalade which he'd placed on the magic table only a few minutes before had disappeared!

He searched hurriedly through the book. There was nothing about making marmalade disappear. Worse still, there was nothing about making it come back again, either. Paddington decided it must be a very powerful spell to make a whole pot vanish into thin air.

He was about to rush outside and tell the others when he thought better of it. It might be a good trick to do in the evening, especially if he could persuade Mrs. Bird to give him another jar. He went out into the kitchen and waved his wand a few times in Mrs. Bird's direction, just to make sure.

" I'll give you ABRACADABRA," said Mrs. Bird, pushing him out again. " And be careful with that stick or you'll have someone's eye out."

Paddington returned to the drawing-room and tried saying his spell backwards. Nothing happened, so he started reading the next chapter of the instruction

118

book, which was called THE MYSTERY OF THE DIS-
APPEARING EGG.

"I shouldn't have thought you needed any book
to tell you that," said Mrs. Bird at lunch time, as
Paddington told them all about it. "The way you
gobble your food is nobody's business."

"Well," said Mr. Brown, "so long as you don't
try sawing anyone in half this evening, I don't
mind."

"I was only joking," he added hurriedly, as
Paddington turned an inquiring gaze on him. Never-
theless, as soon as lunch was over, Mr. Brown hurried
down the garden and locked up his tools. With
Paddington there was no sense in taking chances.

As it happened he had no cause to worry, for
Paddington had far too many things on his mind what
with one thing and another. The whole family were
there for tea as well as Mr. Gruber. Several other
people came along too, including the Browns' next
door neighbour, Mr. Curry. The last named was a
most unwelcome visitor. "Just because there's a free
tea," said Mrs. Bird. "I think it's disgusting, taking
the crumbs off a young bear's plate like that. He's
not even been invited!"

"He'll have to look slippy if he gets any crumbs
off Paddington's plate," said Mr. Brown. "All the
same, it *is* a bit thick, after all the things he's said in
the past. And not even bothering to wish him many
happy returns."

Mr. Curry had a reputation in the neighbourhood for meanness and for poking his nose into other people's business. He was also very badtempered, and was always complaining about the least little thing which met with his disapproval. In the past that had often included Paddington, which was why the Browns had not invited him to the party.

But even Mr. Curry had no cause to complain about the tea. From the huge birthday cake down to the last marmalade sandwich, everyone voted it was

the best tea they had ever had. Paddington himself was so full he had great difficulty in mustering enough breath to blow out the candle. But at last he managed it without singeing his whiskers, and everyone, including Mr. Curry, applauded and wished him a happy birthday.

" And now," said Mr. Brown, when the noise had died down. " If you'll all move your seats back, I think Paddington has a surprise for us."

While everyone was busy moving their seats to one side of the room, Paddington disappeared into the drawing-room and returned carrying his conjuring outfit. There was a short delay while he erected his magic table and adjusted the mystery box, but soon all was ready. The lights were turned off except for a standard lamp and Paddington waved his wand for quiet.

" Ladies and gentlemen," he began, consulting his instruction book, " my next trick is impossible! "

" But you haven't done one yet," grumbled Mr. Curry.

Ignoring the remark, Paddington turned over the page. " For this trick," he said. " I shall require an egg."

" Oh dear," said Mrs. Bird, as she hurried out to the kitchen, " I know something dreadful is going to happen."

Paddington placed the egg in the centre of his magic table and covered it with a handkerchief. He muttered ABRACADABRA several times and then hit the handkerchief with his wand.

Mr. and Mrs. Brown looked at each other. They were both thinking of their carpet. " Hey presto! "

said Paddington, and pulled the handkerchief away. To everyone's surprise the egg had completely disappeared.

"Of course," said Mr. Curry, knowledgeably, above the applause, "it's all done by sleight of paw. But very good though, for a bear. Very good indeed. Now make it come back again!"

Feeling very pleased with himself, Paddington took his bow and then felt in the secret compartment behind the table. To his surprise he found something much larger than an egg. In fact . . . it was a jar of marmalade. It was the one that had disappeared that very morning! He displayed it in his paw; the applause for this trick was even louder.

"Excellent," said Mr. Curry, slapping his knee. "Making people think he was going to find an egg, and it was a jar of marmalade all the time. Very good indeed!"

Paddington turned over a page. "And now," he announced, flushed with success, "the disappearing trick!" He took a bowl of Mrs. Brown's best flowers and placed them on the dining-table alongside his mystery box. He wasn't very happy about this trick, as he hadn't had time to practise it, and he wasn't at all sure how the mystery box worked or even where you put the flowers to make them disappear.

He opened the door in the back of the box and then poked his head round the side. "I shan't be a minute," he said, and then disappeared from view again.

The audience sat in silence. " Rather a slow trick, this one," said Mr. Curry, after a while.

" I hope he's all right," said Mrs. Brown. " He seems very quiet."

" Well, he can't have gone far," said Mr. Curry. " Let's try knocking." He got up, knocked loudly on the box, and then put his ear to it. " I can hear someone calling," he said. " It sounds like Paddington. I'll try again." He shook the box and there was an answering thump from inside.

" I think he's shut himself in," said Mr. Gruber. He too knocked on the box and called out, "Are you all right, Mr. Brown? "

" NO! " said a small and muffled voice. " It's all dark and I can't read my instruction book."

" Quite a good trick," said Mr. Curry, some while later, after they had prised open Paddington's mystery box with a penknife. He helped himself to some biscuits. " The disappearing bear. Very unusual! But I still don't see what the flowers were for."

Paddington looked at him suspiciously, but Mr. Curry was far too busy with the biscuits.

" For my next trick," said Paddington, " I would like a watch."

" Are you sure? " asked Mrs. Brown, anxiously. " Wouldn't anything else do? "

Paddington consulted his instruction book. " It says a watch," he said, firmly.

Mr. Brown hurriedly pulled his sleeve down over his left wrist. Unfortunately, Mr. Curry, who was in an unusually good mood after his free tea, stood up and offered his. Paddington took it gratefully and placed it on the table. " This is a jolly good trick," he said, reaching down into his box and pulling out a small hammer.

He covered the watch with a handkerchief and then hit it several times. Mr. Curry's expression froze. " I hope you know what you're doing, young bear," he said.

Paddington looked rather worried. Having turned over the page he'd just read the ominous words, " It is necessary to have a second watch for this trick." Gingerly, he lifted up a corner of the handkerchief. Several cogs and some pieces of glass rolled across the table. Mr. Curry let out a roar of wrath.

" I think I forgot to say ABRACADABRA," faltered Paddington.

" ABRACADABRA! " shouted Mr. Curry, beside himself with rage. " ABRACADABRA! " He held up the remains of his watch. " Twenty years I've had this watch, and now look at it! This will cost someone a pretty penny! "

Mr. Gruber took out an eyeglass and examined the watch carefully. " Nonsense," he said, coming to

Paddington's rescue. " It's one you bought from me for five shillings six months ago! You ought to be ashamed of yourself, telling lies in front of a young bear! "

" Rubbish! " spluttered Mr. Curry. He sat down heavily on Paddington's chair. " Rubbish! I'll give you . . ." his voice trailed away and a peculiar expression came over his face. " I'm sitting on something," he said. " Something wet and sticky! "

" Oh dear," said Paddington. " I expect it's my disappearing egg. It must have reappeared! "

Mr. Curry grew purple in the face. " I've never been so insulted in my life," he said. " Never! " He turned at the door and waved an accusing finger at the company. " It's the last time I shall ever come to one of *your* birthday parties! "

" Henry," said Mrs. Brown, as the door closed behind Mr. Curry, " you really oughtn't to laugh."

Mr. Brown tried hard to keep a straight face. " It's no good," he said, bursting out. " I can't help it."

" Did you see his face when all the cogs rolled out? " said Mr. Gruber, his face wet with tears.

" All the same," said Mr. Brown, when the laughter had died down. " I think perhaps you ought to try something a little less dangerous next time, Paddington."

" How about that card trick you were telling me about, Mr. Brown? " asked Mr. Gruber. " The one where you tear up a card and make it come out of someone's ear."

"Yes, that sounds a nice quiet one," said Mrs. Brown. "Let's see that."

"You wouldn't like another disappearing trick?" asked Paddington, hopefully.

"Quite sure, dear," said Mrs. Brown.

"Well," said Paddington, rummaging in his box, "it's not very easy doing card tricks when you've only got paws, but I don't mind trying."

He offered a pack of cards to Mr. Gruber, who solemnly took one from the middle and then memorised it before replacing the card. Paddington waved his wand over the pack several times and then withdrew a card. He held up the seven of spades. "Was this it?" he said to Mr. Gruber.

Mr. Gruber polished his glasses and stared. "You know," he said, "I do believe it was!"

"I bet all the cards are the same," whispered Mr. Brown to his wife.

"Ssh!" said Mrs. Brown. "I thought he did it very well."

"This is the difficult bit," said Paddington, tearing it up. "I'm not very sure about this part." He put the pieces under his handkerchief and tapped them several times with the wand.

"Oh!" said Mr. Gruber, rubbing the side of his head. "I felt something go pop in my ear just then. Something cold and hard." He felt in his ear. "Why,

I do believe . . ." he held up a shining round object to the audience. " It's a sovereign! My birthday present for Paddington! Now I wonder how it got in there? "

" Oooh! " said Paddington, as he proudly examined it. " I didn't expect that. Thank you very much, Mr. Gruber."

" Well," said Mr. Gruber. " It's only a small present I'm afraid, Mr. Brown. But I've enjoyed the little chats we've had in the mornings. I look forward to them very much and, er," he cleared his throat and looked around, " I'm sure we all hope you have many more birthdays! "

When the chorus of agreement had died down, Mr. Brown rose and looked at the clock. " And now," he said, " it's long past all our bedtimes, most of all yours, Paddington, so I suggest we all do a disappearing trick now."

" I wish," said Paddington, as he stood at the door waving everyone good-bye, " I wish my Aunt Lucy could see me now. She'd feel very pleased."

" You'll have to write and tell her all about it, Paddington," said Mrs. Brown, as she took his paw. " But in the morning," she added hastily. " You've got clean sheets, remember."

" Yes," said Paddington. " In the morning. I expect if I did it now I'd get ink over the sheets or something. Things are always happening to me."

"You know, Henry," said Mrs. Brown, as they watched Paddington go up the stairs to bed, looking rather sticky and more than a little sleepy, "it's nice having a bear about the house."

15(55)

698032

J
BON

Bond, Michael

A bear called
Paddington

In Best Books 6th ed 1990
In Children's Cat. 17th ed 1996

$12.95

DATE			

92
94 OCT 1 9 1990 98
93   97
      95
92
91